KAMALA

KAMALA:

A STORY OF HINDU LIFE

Mrs. S. SATTHIANADHAN

GYAN

Published by

Gyan Publishing House
5, Ansari Road
Daryaganj, New Delhi-110002
Phone: 011-47034999, 9811692060
E-mail: books@gyanbooks.com

Distribution Network
gyanbooks.com
India, USA, Canada, UK, Australia, France

ISBN: 978-81-212-8744-9 (PB)
First Published, 1894

2nd Impression 2023

Printed at: Gyan Press, Delhi.

KAMALA
Author: Mrs. S. Satthianadhan

KAMALA:

A STORY OF HINDU LIFE.

Krupa Sattianadhan

KAMALA:

A STORY OF HINDU LIFE

BY

MRS. S. SATTHIANADHAN,

Author of "Saguna."

WITH

AN INTRODUCTORY MEMOIR

BY

MRS. H. B. GRIGG.

Madras:
SRINIVASA, VARADACHARI & CO.
MRS. RADHABAI ATMARAM SAGOON, BOMBAY.

1894.

MADRAS:
PRINTED BY SRINIVASA, VARADACHARI & CO.,
MOUNT ROAD.

To

Her Excellency Lady Wenlock,

THIS BOOK

is respectfully dedicated,

In accordance with the wishes of the authoress, who felt greatly cheered and encouraged, during the writing of it, by the kind interest manifested in her humble literary efforts, by Her Ladyship.

MEMOIR OF

Krupabai Satthianadhan.

UNLIKE Toru Dutt of Bengal, who has been called her prototype, the authoress of Kamala lived to see her literary efforts recognised. Now that she has passed away, the Indian Press has expressed the pride which her countrymen feel in her and their sorrow for her early death.

Her writings seem even better known to English than to Indian readers, some of them having been reviewed in flattering terms in the leading English Journals. Her Majesty the Queen Empress had recently accepted a copy of "Saguna" and was graciously pleased to request that any other work by the authoress should be sent to her.

It might almost seem that Krupabai Satthianadhan is already too well known to need that her story should be told except as she herself has told it in "Saguna." But the final chapters of her life remain to be written, and to judge of her as an authoress and as a woman, we must view her surroundings and the position of her countrywomen when her life began.

Thirty years ago female education had made but little progress in India. Missionaries were still bribing little girls to come to school with offers of food or clothing as they had been obliged to bribe boys a generation before. The great mass of the women of India were completely uneducated, and their position was becoming more and more unenviable as the education of men progressed and the difference between the intellectual status of the men and of the women in a household became greater.

There is a good deal to show that in Vedic times women had lived a free and healthy life, sharing often in the pursuits and interests of their husbands. They seem even to have had some literary skill and to have composed hymns and songs. But the age in which they lived is remote and its history too much mixed up with myth and legend to be trustworthy. Such are the heroines in the Great Indian Epics, the Mahabharata and the Ramayana.

In historic times one or two bright instances like that of the Queen of Beechapore alone occur to relieve the dim twilight in which women—Hindu and Mohammadan alike—lived for many hundreds of years.

But when the work of enlightenment of women consequent on the spread of English education amongst men began, it progressed steadily. For some time it had been recognised that an extraordinary state of things had been brought about by educating one half of the Indian people and leaving the other half in comparative ignorance. But obstacles such as prejudice on the one hand and timidity on the other, stood in the way.

"To these difficulties may be added the belief, perhaps more widely felt than expressed, that the general education of women means a social revolution the extent of which cannot be foreseen. Native gentlemen, advanced and enlightened enough in ordinary matters, are hampered by the dread that when the women of the country begin to be educated, and to learn independence, harassing times are in store for them. They may thoroughly allow that when the process has been completed, the nation will rise in intelligence, in character, and in all the graces of life. But they are none the less apprehensive that while the process of educatian is going on, while the lessons of emancipation are being learnt and stability has not yet been reached, while, in short, society is slowly struggling to adjust itself to the new conditions, the period of transition will be marked by the loosening of social ties, the upheaval of customary ways, and by prolonged, and severe domestic embarrassment. There is, it is true, an advanced section of the community that is entirely out of sympathy with these views."

So wrote Sir Alfred Croft, the Director of Public Instruction in Bengal, as late as 1886—when already by the liberal policy of the Government a great deal had been achieved in the advancement of female education.

By degrees, the desire for this education has grown and the demand for it is now gradually coming healthily from within, needing, in the great centres of civilisation at least, much less fostering from without.

It is difficult to realize the beginnings of any great movement, to trace the steps by which it has advanced, and to divest it of features which are the outcome of later times. This difficulty increases when it is a question of comparing such movements in countries and races as different as are those of the east and of the west. Still it is interesting to note how much this work of enlightenment has in common with a movement of a similar kind which began in England about the middle of the last century. An impetus was then given to the education of women in England by such writers as Hannah More, Mary Lamb and Miss Edgeworth, and in India, a century later, by some devoted Missionaries scattered throughout the country, especially by those connected with the Free Church of Scotland. Though in India, women undoubtedly started from a much lower and from an essentially different platform, in both cases this impetus not only stirred the springs of intellectual activity and individual culture, but it has also made women's hearts beat faster. The severest critics of the "New Woman" must admit that deeper culture has in the long run led to wider sympathies, and that wider sympathies have opened out new and broader fields for philanthropic and useful work,—work which is making the lives of thousands of women happier as well as better. A long list of noble English women rises in one's mind—names too well known to be repeated here. To one England owes the scientific care of her sick and wounded soldiers: others have toiled for the poor, the ignorant, and the oppressed. In song and in story, women have poured forth the same refrain in wise and true sympathy with all that is highest and best. These were the pioneers; others are following them,—in the main, upwards and onwards, though a few may fail and some may have brought ridicule on themselves, and some have not been "loveable though they deserved to be honored and thankfully remembered."

India too has had her pioneers; alas! her martyrs also in the cause of women's education and enlightenment. The feverish thirst for learning and for expression which has seized upon some of her most gifted daughters has more than once led to failing health and even to early death. Superstitious and ignorant people are ever ready to "point a moral and adorn a tale" with the story of their mistaken ardour, and to quote them as proving that, in India at least, women are incapable of bearing any prolonged mental strain.

The history of these women is intensely pathetic, and Lady Dufferin has well said in her Introduction to "Sketches of some Distinguished Indian women," by Mrs. E. F. Chapman, "One might perhaps have feared that women who had had to break the hard and fast rules of caste and custom would have lost their more loveable characteristic in the struggle ; but one rises from the perusal of their biographies with as much affection for the woman as admiration for the student."

This is indeed most true. Indian women with sweet reasonableness seem to have avoided the especial failings of pioneers. Still the women whom Mrs. Chapman has selected for her sketches are one and all instances of how much there is in common in the waves of thought which have stirred the women of the East and the women of the West. Rather is it not one and the same wave—a wave of hopeful unrest, of eager longing for truth and of unselfish enthusiasm. Every one of the names which stand out conspicuously among the women of India are the names of those whose dearest wish has been or still is to serve their fellow country-women. They are all, whether Christians or of other cults, permeated with humanistic and altruistic ideas. One of the earliest to be affected by this feeling was Toru Dutt, the gifted poetess. She, like many other Hindu ladies, owed much to her mother. "In every case," as Mrs. Chapman observes, "the work of education and enlightenment has been begun in the previous generation." She owed much too to her sojourn in France and in England. But such genius as hers must have found voice in any language and in any land. Some of her sweetest utterances are recollections of stories learnt at her mother's knee, myths which had lost their religious significance as she had learnt to rest in a purer faith, but which retained for her always their poetic beauty. Writing to a French friend, she says, "Quand j'entends ma mère chanter le soir lès vieux chants de notre pays je pleure presque tonjours." Perhaps, however, the following little serenade is more wonderful than any she has written, when it is remembered that the authoress was not twenty and that she wrote in a foreign language.

Still barred thy doors! The far east glows,
The morning wind blows fresh and free.

Should not the hour that wakes the rose
 Awaken also thee!
All look for thee, Love, Light and Song,
Light in the sky deep red above,
Song, in the Lark of pinions strong,
And in my heart, true Love.
Apart we miss our nature's goal,
Why strive to cheat our destinies?
Was not my love made for thy soul?
Thy beauty for mine eyes.
 No longer sleep,
 Oh listen now.
 I wait and weep
 But where art thou?

On her return from England Toru Dutt began to study Sanscrit. "The remaining years of her life" says her biographer, "were spent in the old garden-house in Calcutta, in a feverish dream of intellectual effort and imaginative production. When we consider what she achieved in these forty-five months of seclusion, it is impossible to wonder that the frail and hectic body succumbed under so excessive a strain."

Krupabai Satthianadhan too died young. She was only thirty-two when she passed away on the 3rd of August last. But short as her life has been she has left behind writings which will cause her name to live as the first of Indian women novelists. Those who loved her still see her, through a mist of tears, stepping fearlessly onward in untrodden paths,—the slight form enveloped in the graceful costume of her country, its veil drawn Madonna-wise over the well-shaped head framing her fair refined face.

In her were strangely blended all that is sweetest in womanhood and an overmastering will and courage, —a courage which helped her to bear long periods of weakness and of suffering with cheerful patience,—her clear intellect and vivid imagination seeming to triumph over her pain and to lift her above it into a world of her own.

Krupabai was the thirteenth child of Haripunt and Radhabai, who were the first Brahmin converts to Christianity in the Bombay Presidency. She was born at Ahmednugger on the 14th February 1862. The great struggle of their lives, their conversion, was over before any of their children were born and Haripunt had made his choice and had embarked on a life of earnest self-denial as a Christian Missionary.

It is difficult to over-rate the sacrifice which a Brahmin makes when he renounces the religion of his forefathers. It implies the giving up of friends, position, wealth and of almost everything which men hold dear. Some of the most striking writings in "Saguna" describe Haripunt's conflict with himself. "One evening in the gloaming," his daughter tells us, "and amidst the fading glory of the Western Sun, all that he had read came before him with a new and forcible light. He saw the God-man now stooping by the side of the despised blind beggar with a word of comfort for him, now healing the sick, now consoling the grieved, now raising the fallen, with those magic words, 'Thy Sins be forgiven thee, go in peace,' now with Divine light penetrating into the inmost recesses of the hearts of those whom the world looked upon as past redemption, and laying bare to hypocrites the hidden spark of goodness and real love there. By the side of these rose other pictures—Christ's communion with God on the mountain-top; His striking presence in Bethany surrounded by those whom he loved; His grief by the side of the dead; the God-voice piercing the shadows of the grave and the unknown regions beyond, and demanding the dead back to life; the scene on the Mount of Olives when with His prophetic eye He saw the distant future, foretold the fall of the temple and depicted those fearful scenes that would follow; and last of all the scene on Calvary rose vividly before the mind of Harichandra. He hid his face and groaned: "Such love! I will follow Thee, my Saviour. Here before my country, my home, my people, I give myself up to Thee a whole-hearted sacrifice. Accept me My God. All I have I leave to follow Thee."

Then when the worst was over, Radhabai had still to be persuaded to leave her people and to join him. One must pity the poor child-wife when she learns the truth and finds herself entrapped, as she thinks, into a Christian Mission house.

"This was the Padre Sahib's house and she had entered it, she a Brahmin. What pollution! What degradation! A time of anguish followed. In her first impulse she tried to push open the door and shook the bars of the window; but when she found herself powerless, she sat down on the floor quivering with anger and with the sense of some great wrong done to her. * * * * * * * * *
The gentle Radha was for the time changed into an avenging angel who shot her glances and words with withering scorn at her husband. * * * * * * * * *
He could only say: 'Rest content Radha I am doing all this for your good.' His heart went out to her though her words beat on him with untold agony. But when with tragic earnestness she threw her jewels at his feet and asked him if it was money he needed and falling at his feet piteously entreated him to run away from the place and take her to Tai Bai (her much dreaded mother-in-law) he could bear it no longer, and went out of the room with a heavy distressed heart."

For some time Radha remained obdurate repelling

all advances from the ladies of the Mission, keeping her fasts and festivals and giving her husband his food outside their house. But at last his forbearance and the kindness of those about her prevailed and her daughter tells us:—"She succumbed to the strong influences of Christianity. It was the silent acquiescence of a gentle nature; and when she came to know more of the religion, she fully appreciated the noble motives that guided her husband's actions of love and charity, his strong confidence in his God, his whole-hearted consecration to his Lord and Master, and at last in the religion which her husband had embraced, she herself found a rich harvest of joy and happiness."

The simple story of their lives from this time and the description of their home with their children about them should be read by all who are inclined to question what Christianity has done for India. Radhabai filled her place well as a wife and mother. Though she never learnt to read herself she seems to have put no barrier in the way of her children's education and to have influenced them and held her own in their esteem by the natural sweetness and strength of her character, her own position in the household being a freer and more influential one than it could ever have been in a Brahmin home.

"Saguna" is essentially an autobiography, though necessarily an idealized one, and therefore we cannot do better than to follow in it the early years of Krupabai's life tracing the influences which helped to form her character. She thus describes the home of her childhood.

"A large family grew up around Harichandra and Radha. The Christian life in that house was of a simple apostolic type, The children knew no luxuries nor hankered after any. The little ones tumbled about in coarse garments which Radha prepared herself. They often displayed somewhat ridiculous combinations of English and Native dress, for comfort was studied rather than effect. The girls knew nothing of ornaments or jewels, and the boys put their hands to manual labour as readily as they took to study. There was an absence of false shame and pride, which imparted a certain innocence and freshness to their manner and behaviour. Simplicity, truthfulness, piety and the habit of self-reliance were inculcated. On the other hand, anything like duplicity, obstinacy, or levity was severely punished."

Haripunt's eldest daughter, who is living still, resembled him in many ways. We are told that she was his friend and companion. Her education, received in a European Christian family, where she was treated almost like a daughter, fitted her to take his place in guiding and teaching her brothers and sisters, when her father died in 1858. Her influence and that of an elder brother, who died while still a young man, did much in forming Krupabai's character. The little girl seems to have shown unusual intellectual powers at an early age. Her thirst for knowledge made her press for permission to learn with her brothers, or at least, to be allowed to remain in the room when they studied, whilst they, boy-like, objected to the presence of a girl especially as she frequently corrected their sums or gave right answers when theirs were wrong. But they never succeeded in banishing her to the kitchen fire, "the right place for a girl," and, by degrees, became proud of their little sister's attainments. Like Mrs. Carlyle whose successful declining of the noun *penna* from under the table gained her the privilege of learning Latin, Krupabai's pertinacity triumphed in the end. The elder brother always stood her friend. He saw the depth in the child's character and she looked up to him and reverenced his earnest devoted spirit. The two enjoyed together the wild scenery of the Upper Deccan where the family removed for her brother Bhasker's health. Young as she was, Krupabai seems to have bent and swayed to every changing mood of nature around her. She thus describes their last morning on the hill tops before returning to the city home:

"I remember well the last day when Bashkar and I got up while the stars were still shining and stole to the mountain heights to have a last look at the dear place. There was nothing to be seen at first as far as the eye could reach except small and great hills and peaks all round; but soon the scene changed. As we ascended the hill in front of our house we seemed to be leaving the world, and piercing the region of the unknown, so thick was the mist around us, and when we reached the highest point we were startled by the dim majesty and grandeur that burst upon us. We seemed to be looking down upon mortals below in another world. The shadowy cloudland, dark and gloomy, like a large bird with spreading wings, hovered overhead and the great world, sleeping in mist, lay below in its purity and whiteness like a huge sea stretched at our feet. It was the silence of eternity linked to the world for a moment. A soft starry dreamland light enwrapt and overspread all. Above, the neighbouring peaks, distant and dark, mysteriously loomed like fingers pointing to heaven. The strangely transformed world, the heavenly beauty and purity of the scene bound us fast and when I looked up my brother seemed strangely excited. He turned to me and said; 'It was in this place with such a scene before me some years ago that I determined that my life should be pure and holy. Oh how our lives are wasted. Promise to me that yours will be devoted to God's glory.' We were alone, alone with God on the mountain top and we fell on our knees and prayed."

But the son soon followed the father, and this time Krupabai's heart was sorely tried. For many months she did not recover from the shock of his death, and her health suffered materially.

Partly in the hope of arousing her, she was sent

first to study with some Lady Missionaries and then to school at the Zenana Mission in Bombay. There it was found that instead of being, as she feared, more backward than the other scholars of her own age, she was too far in advance of them to be placed in any of the classes. She was therefore allowed to pursue her own course of study. She thus fell under the influence of an American lady doctor,—a person of much originality and force of character and this circumstance led eventually to her choice of a profession.

Krupabai's remarkable talents and her desire to study medicine induced her English friends to think of sending her to England to complete her education there. She herself was most anxious to go, but it was feared that her constitution was not sufficiently strong to bear the strain of severe study in a climate which, to her, would have been most trying. The Medical College in Madras had just then opened its doors to women,—the first school of medicine in India to adopt this liberal policy,—and her friends decided to send her there. She accordingly left Bombay unaccompanied by any friend or guardian and was received in Madras by the father of her future husband, the Rev. W. T. Satthianadhan. She could not have been placed in better hands. Mr. Satthianadhan was a much respected clergyman and earnest Missionary,—one of the earliest undergraduates students of the Presidency and a Fellow of the University of Madras. He had been honored by the Archbishop of Canterbury with the degree of Bachelor of Divinity. His influence and that of his excellent wife and daughters was for many years a power for good among the community of which he was the head. A tender affection sprang up between them and Krupabai, and she passed a happy year in their house, working steadily and attending lectures at the Medical College. She has, in "Saguna," described her reception there, when the whole body of students rose as she entered and cheered the delicate looking girl, the first Indian lady who had joined their ranks. At the end of a year she had won several prizes and stood first in every subject except Chemistry. Some envious feeling might, not unnaturally, have been aroused by the high praise bestowed on her in the class room by the professors but, to their honor be it spoken, her fellow-students appear to have always behaved kindly and generously towards her. This may have been partly due to her unassuming and gentle demeanour. Writing of her, the other day, a former Head of the Medical College says : "I always thought her one of the sweetest characters I ever knew. She was so gentle, thoughtful and intelligent. As a worker she was a conscientious and untiring student."

Unfortunately her fragile frame was not strong in proportion to the ardent soul within it, and when the excitement of the examination was over, her nerve forsook her, and her health broke down completely. Nor was she ever strong enough again to resume her medical studies. It was one of the dreams of her life to complete them in England but this wish was never fulfilled. Her genius found another and a different field as will be seen.

In 1881 Krupabai met the son of her friend and host in Madras. Mr. Samuel Satthianadhan had just then returned from England, after passing nearly four years at Cambridge where he had distinguishd himself and had graduated with honors. It must have been a surprise to him to find, as Krupabai's shyness and physical weakness wore off, and her bright intellect could assert itself, the depth of thought and of enthusiasm that lay beneath that quiet exterior. To her it was new life to hear the subjects of the day discussed by one fresh from the homes of thought and learning, who still could be true to his own country and his own people, and who was ready to share her schemes for their benefit.

It was only natural that they should mutually attract one another. It may have cost Krupabai an effort to give up the freer life of intellectual pursuits which she had sketched out for herself, and which had been her ambition even in her school-days. "How hard," she says, "it seemed to my mind that marriage should be the goal of a woman's ambition and that she should spend her days in the light trifles of a home life, live to dress, to look pretty, and never know the joy of independence and intellectual work." But, in the end, she found that love and intellectual life are not incompatible and her best work was eventually done in the home to which her husband took her. Krupabai had once before dedicated her life to God, when alone with her brother on the mountains. This brother, her best guide and friend, had been taken from her. Again, in the full bloom of her girlhood and of maturer thought and feeling, she realised what it was to find in another heart the echo of her own best aspirations, and to start afresh with a companion whose goal was the same and whose "feet were also planted on the Rock of Ages." "There was no fear now," she says, "no losing one's way. Let darkness come, let the whole world be blotted out from view, darkness and night would have no terror for us. Christ was ours. God was ours. Heaven was ours, and our lives were to be one full and joyous song."

So far I have allowed Krupabai to tell much of her own story. Those who wish for more details will find them in "Saguna."

It was whilst she was a student in the Medical College that I first knew her, and that acquaintance ripened into friendship, when, after her marriage, she lived for nearly two years near us at Ootacamund, where her husband was the Headmaster of the Breeks' Memorial School. Krupabai's health had improved and her bright spirit revelled in the glorious scenery, the exhilarating air and the lovely flowers of the Nilgiris. They reminded her of that mountainous region of the Deccan where she had spent a portion of her childhood.

Here she began at once to seek out ways of being useful. She spent many hours in the week in Zenanas, and in the Hobart School for native girls, where she superintended and improved the teaching. She also started a little school for the hitherto neglected Mohammadan girls in Ootacamund. This school has since developed into a fairly large and very useful one under the auspices of the C. M. S. Mission.

Her first attempt at writing was an article contributed about this time to the *South India Observer*. It was called "A Visit to the Todas," and appeared under the *nom de plume* of an Indian lady. This was followed by several others chiefly descriptive of the scenery of the Hills. These articles attracted attention by their truthful and vivid delineation of nature and life.

In 1884 Mr. Satthianadhan was appointed to a new charge in Rajahmundry and she accompanied him there. The climate does not seem to have agreed with her. After a few months she broke a blood-vessel very unexpectedly and this was followed by a long and dangerous illness which left her a complete invalid during the rest of her stay,—a period of about a year. She contributed articles to the "National Indian Journal" at this time and to other papers and magazines. The following year was spent in Kumbaconam,—the educational centre of the wealthy Tanjore District. There Krupabai's health began to improve. Her pen was constantly at work and she seems to have begun to take a delight in studying the people about her. No one was too poor or too humble to interest her. She loved to gather "all sorts and conditions" of people around her sofa and to listen to the story of their joys and sorrows. Then probably she first became conscious of her talent as a story-teller, though she was always very distrustful of her own powers. She certainly tried her hand at versification and attained to some facility in thus expressing her thoughts, which were always full of poetry and of devotion. But the exigencies of English Metre were a difficulty to her which she did not overcome until much later.

In 1886 Mr. Satthianadhan was appointed Assistant

to the Director of Public Instruction, and afterwards to the Chair of Logic and Philosophy in the Presidency College, which necessitated their living in Madras. About this time Krupabai was persuaded by a friend, as well as by her husband, to write something beyond the limits of a magazine article. She wisely began by describing what she knew best,—the scenes of her childhood—out of this "Saguna" grew.

Its freshness and originality give it an unusual charm, and there is a vividness and power in some of the scenes which makes them very real. The reader is carried along by the strong individuality of the writer and those chapters which have perhaps called down most criticism are in some respects those which leave the clearest pictures on the mind. Krupabai's education had been unlike that of most girls of her own race or of ours. Christianity had been taught to her with an apostolic simplicity utterly free from the Shibboleths and conventionalities of the nineteenth century. As regards secular subjects she had leant on no system and probably was ignorant of some things which most children are taught, whilst in other respects she was considerably in advance of girls of her own age. So that when asked by her teachers to "parse" a word she had no idea what was required of her, though her knowledge of grammar made her quite equal to the task when the term, new to her, was explained. Mind and body had developed unevenly and when she joined the Mission School in Bombay there was undoubtedly, as is often the case with clever and delicate girls at that age, something of the ugly duckling about her. Precocious in mind and thought and terribly in earnest, she was a prey to self-consciousness and to an almost hysterical over-sensitiveness. The discipline there was exactly what she required and after a few misunderstandings and some amusing little "scenes" she and her teachers understood one another.

Wonderful as her grasp of English is it fails her occasionally when she wishes to satirise and make her strokes far heavier than she intends. In like manner the humourous passages sometimes miss their point. This is particularly the case in her account of the Christian village. She wished only to describe its quaintness and some of the drawbacks incident to the collecting of poor and very ignorant converts in communities where they were not under careful supervision. Unfortunately she has been misunderstood, and by those especially whose cause she most wished to serve. It is only fair to her memory that this should be explained. She herself was a standing example of the benefit of a Christian training. Could there be a more charming picture than the one which she has drawn of her own home,—the father sincere, earnest, enthusiastic and self-sacrificing; the mother sweet and gentle, with all the instincts of the Brahman race, freed from its selfish exclusiveness, and developing in the freer, clearer air of a Christian household,—a household, where no despotic mother-in-law is a terror to the wife and mother, and where the women, young and old, may profit by the society and conversation of the father and his friends, unrestrained by cramping and narrowing native customs. Perhaps, however, the subject of this memoir was at her best when describing scenery. She loved nature with the love of an artist and of a poet. Her own nature is stirred to its depths by the grandeur of some of its moods and this when she was a mere child. The power to paint in words which moved her so much was probably increased by her love of English poetry and the extent of her reading. Here is her description of her first experiences of natural scenery:

"My whole being took a great bound, as it were, as the wide expanse of land and sky unfolded itself to my view. I felt the freedom of nature; nothing seemed too great to attempt here; all was on a grand scale. The distant hills had caught the skies. Why! I felt that I could mount and catch them too. I went bounding everywhere and was filled with new life and spirits. After some days I became somewhat sobered, and my elder brother Bhasker promised to take me to a very wild and rocky place. It was on a dewy morning that we went out on this eagerly looked-for walk. The half risen sun was still veiled by the mists and clouds. There was a rich tint of colour on the wreaths of mist overhanging the rocks and hills. The mild light of the dawn had not yet penetrated into the densely wooded haunts and the rocky caves of this hilly country. It was still dark and dim, and only the outlines of the trees and rocks could be discerned, which gave a weird shadowy appearance to the whole scene. The newly awakened birds were all life and merriment. A loud twitter filled the whole place, as the birds kept answering each other from tree to tree. The morning wind, the thin light freshening wind, came along the hills and through the trees in soft and gentle puffs, and we walked together, hand in hand, up and down the mountain path. I was hushed and speechless; the sight, so new, thrilled me with wonder. The mountain path with its loose stones moss-grown and dark, the trees loaded with foliage, the twisted gnarled trunks springing from the midst of granite rocks and stones, the huge serpentine creepers swinging overhead, and over it all the faint glimmering light of dawn,—all this formed a picture too full of living beauty, light and shade, to be ever forgotten. We ascended a little rocky eminence, and were looking at the wonders round us, the mists and the shadows, and the play of the light over all, when suddenly the scene changed, and the sun emerged from behind a huge rock. In a moment the whole place was bathed in light. Did the birds make a louder noise or was the echo stronger, for I thought I heard, with the advent of light, quite an outburst of song and merriment? My brother, in his usual earnest way, remarked that it is just like this, shadowy, dark, mystic, weird, with superstition and bigotry lurking in every corner, before the light of

Christianity comes into a land. When the sun rises, he said, all the glory of the trees and rocks comes into view, each thing assumes its proper proportions and is drawn out in greater beauty and perfection. So it is when the sunbeams of Christianity dispel the darkness of superstition in a land."

So taught by her brother, Saguna's sympathy with the outer world of beauty suffered from no chilling or depressing influence. It grew and developed until the glancing river met her with a smile, the stars looked down with kindly light on her lonely journey, birds told her their tales of love and praise and the glory of the western sky lifted her whole being into a higher atmosphere. "There on those heights I should like to be, there, above the clouds, in the midst of the light or nowhere at all."

Along with much beautiful description of scenery, the book contains some keen analysis of character. Like many of our own novelists Krupubai was rather silent in society. She loved to listen and to observe, making studies for the characters she has reproduced. No one was too insignificant to interest her. Shortly after her first book was completed and when the last chapter had appeared in the Journal of the *Madras Christian College*, Krupabai's baby was born,—her own Saguna—the treasure which was only lent to its parents for a few short months and nearly cost its mother her life. One feels in reading of the death of Kamala's child that the pen which described her sorrow had been dipped in a mother's tears. Her husband wrote of her at this time "she was never herself after this great loss." Yet she never repined but moved about quietly,—seeking to make herself useful and thus to still the aching at her heart. Her husband took her to Bombay thinking that the sight of her old home and her own people would cheer her. But unfortunately the fatigue of the journey prostrated her completely, and she returned again a complete invalid.

She passed several weeks at a hospital in Madras and derived some temporary benefit from the treatment there. She was told however that the illness from which she suffered was one which must sooner or later prove fatal. This intelligence she received with her usual quiet strength and sweetness.

In the year which followed she was deeply pained by the loss of several near relatives, especially by the death of her husband's mother, and then by that of his father, to both of whom she had been tenderly attached, from the time when they had met her as a timid, shy girl and had made her feel at home in Madras. In spite of ill-health and sorrow, or perhaps to keep her to bear both, she wrote continuously from this time. The history of her father-in-law's conversion, which appeared first, contains some of her best writings. It was followed by some sketches of his wife's life and of the good work in her schools in Madras. Then Krupabai's second story, "Kamala," was begun. The longing for expression must have been strong, for she had thought out some of the chapters whilst in the hospital in Madras, notably the one in which Rukma's husband died of cholera. It was written with feverish eagerness for she feared she might not live to complete it. When too ill to hold a pen she would dictate, and some of the last chapters were dictated to her husband when her temperature was actually at 104°. "Let me show that even a simple Indian girl can do something useful," she pleaded, and this desire was granted to her. She lived to see "Kamala" appear in the same Journal whose Editors had recognized the merit of Saguna.

This earnestness of purpose and the way in which she turned her talents to account in a totally different field, when she found that of medicine barred to her by ill-health, betokened surely something very like genius,—a readiness to do the work nearest to hand and her infinite capacity for taking pains.

In many respects, "Kamala" is an advance upon Krupabai's first novel, though we miss the brightness of "Saguna." There is a plot and the writing is that of a more experienced teller of stories. Still it is now and then a little difficult to follow the thread of the narrative. Its prolonged strain of sadness too reflects the painful effort made by the authoress to complete her task. Her talent is perhaps best shown by the manner in which she has divested herself of the effect of her own Christian surroundings and the ethical reflections which, in "Saguna," seemed to flow naturally from her pen. "Kamala" is, as it professes to be, essentially a tale of Indian life. We rise from its perusal to shake off the dream-like feeling of having been living another life and breathing another atmosphere. We are admitted into the secrets of an Indian household,—the difficulties and the sorrows of a Hindu wife and mother. Happy children we meet every day but from the time when an Indian girl enters her mother-in-law's house her life seems rarely to be a very happy one. She is not imprisoned in a Zenana and denied the blessings of air and exercise, but her life is seemingly too often one of hard work, of misconstruction and of covert rebellion against injustice and domestic repression. She sees very little of her husband and only in very exceptional cases takes any part in his pursuits or is able to converse with him alone. Thus he is powerless to help her, and she gains very little from any culture which he may possess and remains in the same narrow ignorance, which no one attempts to enlighten. Kamala is represented as having learnt from the noble old Sanyasi, her father, to think and to feel, and as one with talents of an unusual order, which made her all the more conscious of the narrow circle in which she moved. A more ordinary woman would have hungered less for love and sympathy, would have contented herself with trying to hoard up jewels, and thus lay up a little store against the dark hour, when a cruel fate might make her that saddest of sad beings,—an Indian widow.

Krupabai says:—

"Blame not the poor Indian woman for her love of jewellery, she strives and toils hard to put by a few rupees out of the money allotted to her by her husband for home expenses, and invests the money in jewels. She knows well that they are the only things that will not be taken away from her at her husband's death, or when any trouble or calamity overtakes the family. The jewels are hers whatever may happen to the other property. She sees her future independence in them, or at least has the consolation that she will have something to fall back upon in times of distress. It is a hard wrench when she is obliged to part with one of them. Life is not so dear as these jewels are; for what is the use of living?—she argues within herself,—to be trampled on by others, and to slave for others. Such feelings are purely Hindu and are the outcome of wrongs committed for generations on the poor unprotected Hindu woman."

Almost unknown to herself Kamala had higher

ideals and aspirations. The passionate sorrow and sense of humiliation which drove her, when convinced of her husband's cruelty and faithlessness, to fly, with her baby into the dark night are touching in the extreme.

So too are the dawnings of hope and faith which the stars and the silence of the night seem to teach her. Events are crowded into the last chapters of Kamala. It is natural that it should be so. Still the death of Kamala's child is most pathetically told and her lullaby is the most finished of Krupabai's attempt in verse. She has shown throughout, but especially in the purified Hinduism of the old Sanyasi, whose character is powerfully drawn, and in Kamala's renunciation of the happiness offered to her, that she could enter into and value that spontaneous lifting of the soul by which men and women of every religion and every nationality "are bound about the feet of God." The descriptions of scenery are as beautiful as in "Saguna" and there is some keen analysis of character. But to fairly guage the mind of the authoress the two should be compared,—the story of Christian life and the story of Hindu life.

In her autobiography she has shown, sometimes it would almost seem unconsciously, what a higher culture and a purer faith can achieve in her country. She brings into strong contrast the ignorance and superstition of Kamala's home and the equally simple but happy and enlightened atmosphere of her own home and surroundings. Her sense of humour and her truthfulness led her to paint the picture as it appeared to her. But the touches of satire, here and there, are not the straws which show the way the wind blows but the light spray tossed back by the breeze when the tide is setting full in a contrary direction. Did we need it, the story of Kamala would confirm this. It must also prove that Krupabai's love for her countrywomen remained as strong as if she had not been divided from them by a different faith and a higher culture. The character of Kamala is purely Hindu and it is drawn with a loving hand. Young, beautiful and intelligent, she needed only to have seen the light to have recognised and absorbed it. There is surely no character in fiction more pure. Once, only once, "in the midst of her misery," we are told, "a wish intruded itself in the deepest and most sacred chamber of her heart,—a wish which made her blush at her boldness and cover her bosom with her hands as if to hide it from herself. Would, she said to herself, that Ganesh had been more like Ramchander. Such a wish, though natural it may seem, was shocking in the extreme to a Hindu girl, who must never allow herself to compare her husband to anybody else." Like Enid, in her patience, Kamala stoops until she can stoop no lower that she may lift a weak and unworthy husband, and, in the end, she puts aside the happiness offered to her that she may be true to his memory and to her ideal of a faithful wife.

"Her religion, crude as it was, had its victory."

This is the key-note of the book. This is what Krupabai seems to say to her people:—"There is a higher light which you have not yet discovered. If it has been revealed to me, I have not forgotten that your lives may still be the highest and the noblest, that we are all feeling after the same God 'though He be not far from every one of us.'"

The greater portion of "Kamala" was written at Conoor in the Nilgiris, whither Krupabai had been taken, in 1893, in the hope that the cool air of the Hills might in some measure restore her strength. She was taken again to Conoor in April last. The change did at first seem to revive her but only temporarily, and though tenderly nursed by her husband and his sister, her health continued to decline, and at one time her life was despaired of. Her cheerfulness seems never to have forsaken her, and her strong faith burnt more brightly as death approached. She lived to return to Madras, but the sudden death of the sister who had tended her was a shock greater than in her feeble state she could bear, and the life which had long hung on a thread ended peacefully on the 8th August 1894. She lies beside her child, in a quiet unlovely cemetery, at Pursewaukam in Madras.

Who can say what Krupabai might have achieved had her life been prolonged, and had her fragile frame been strong in proportion to the soul within it? Her most poetic prose gave promise of the future poetess. Her books though written in a language foreign to her are worthy to take rank among English Fiction for their exquisite description of scenery, their life-like delineation of character, and for the pure and earnest spirit which breathes in every line.

She has interpreted her countrywomen to us as no writer has done before. Seeming to reach a hand to each and to plead to us to study the people about us and to enter more fully into their interests,—into their joys and sorrows, their hopes and fears. Whilst to her country women she must ever be a bright herald beckoning to them to leave their prejudices behind, to learn to understand us better, and to walk on fearlessly in the path of knowledge and of enlightenment in which she has led the way.

Krupabai never sought notoriety, she lived a quiet studious life, though she had many friends both Native and European. Still the home which she shared with her husband was a small centre of intellectual culture and of modern thought. She loved, when health permitted, to meet her friends, and especially shone when, as was frequently the case in Madras, some English lady sought her help in entertaining other Indian ladies. She could on these occasions be as bright and playful as a child.

The freedom of her position as a Christian and the wife of a Christian, her descent from a good Brahman stock, and her great intelligence, sweetness of manner, and breadth of views all helped to give her influence and to add weight to the views she advocated. She will ever be a standing reproach to those who deny the effect of Western teaching and who would meet out grudgingly to Indian women the benefits of Western education.

Her wide and varied reading of English authors resulted in no servile imitation. On the contrary she seems to have absorbed and assimilated the thoughts of the poets she loved, until they became a part of herself and helped to make her what she was.

As an authoress she is singularly truthful, original and courageous. No novelist or story-teller in Southern India, or, as far as I know, in India has achieved so much, either as regards a mastery over our language or in an absolute freedom from imitation or book-making.

From her deep love of nature and her manner of describing it one would have expected to find that Wordsworth was her favorite poet, but although she doubtless was well acquainted with his poems and may have unconsciously reproduced some of his thoughts she seems to have preferred Tennyson, Longfellow, Mrs. Browning and Lewis Morris. The lyrics in *The Princess* she especially loved and Tennyson's last sweet poem :—

> 'Sunset and evening star
> And one clear call for me,'

seems to have been often on her lips before she died.

She took great delight in the writings of George Eliot, and indeed in those of most of our best writers of fiction. Some of Rudyard Kipling's stories and poems she read with pleasure during her last illness.

It had been her intention in her next book to deal with peasant life in India, making her Ayah the heroine of the story. Her sympathy with the poor and perfect simplicity made her well-fitted to be their exponent. She would have thrown herself into their life with the same earnestness that characterized her other writings.

Krupabai Satthianadhan has left no children to follow in her footsteps, but her memory is a precious possession to all true daughters of India. It must fill them with hopes that they may yet produce a beautiful and beneficent literature. It must fill them with gratitude,—a gratitude in which we English women share, for she has taught us to know and to love each other better.

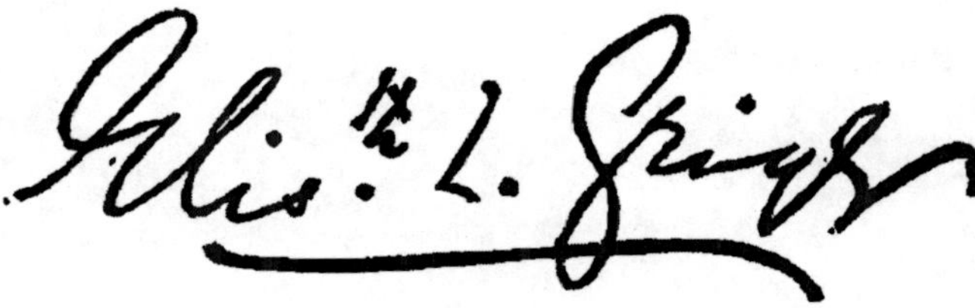

RESIDENCY
TRIVANDRUM,
10*th December* 1894.

KAMALA.

A STORY OF HINDU LIFE.

CHAPTER I.

INDIA may not be a perfect paradise, yet there are in it spots of surpassing beauty and grandeur. The mountainous part of the district of Nassick in the Deccan, where Ganga Godavery takes its rise, is one such spot. Here nature is sublime in its majesty and rugged in its grandeur, here hills rise above hills, some verdure clad, others bare, bleak, and barren, with caves and caverns at their bases through which the waters leap in torrents in the rainy season. Here, not far from the chain of hills that form the glorious Western Ghauts, is situated the sacred city to which I shall give the name Sivagunga.

It is evening and the phantasmagoria of clouds, lit by the setting sun, lies stretched in front covering the great open space that seems an arid desert for miles around. On the one side are old, stunted, weather-beaten trees and stony hills, and on the other may be seen the city of Sivagunga, extending as far as the eye can reach, with its domes and cupolas, its glistening tanks and its dingy houses, touched by the rays of the setting sun. On a little hillock, not far away, are a few trees, which appear to catch and retain the halo of departing light in their branches, and through them glimmers the suffused redness of the sunset sky. In the glowing light between the trees, the form of a little girl may be distinctly seen. It is that of Kamala, the daughter of the old Brahman recluse. She stands by the ruined temple that tops the hillock, her face resting on her hand, and a weary expression in her eyes. She seems to be gazing at the blue expanse of the plain below. At last a sigh is heard, and the girl murmurs:—"Father is nowhere to be seen. Oh! when will he come home?" The great big idol stares at her from the temple and the trees rustle mournfully overhead. Poor girl! her thoughts are hard to express. The old woman, her granny, has been cross, her father is not there to protect her from the anger of the old dame and to hush the noise of the *pujaris** who live close by and who keep constantly wrangling among themselves for the temple money. She knows the road her father is to come by. She has often accompanied him to the city to buy vegetables and grain, returning in the evening through the rice fields, all radiant with glints of shining water between the patches of tender green. On such occasions her own hillock would be recognised by her far away, dark and prominent against the evening sky. And the girl would sit on her father's back with her hands round his neck and wonder whether in the growing dusk the

* Priests.

red light was still in the trees, whether the wind, her friend and play-fellow, was there, and whether the old woman, cross but well-meaning was there too ; and as she would look up she would see the red light glinting among the trees while all around would be darkening. At the welcome light a dart of happiness would pass through her, as if a friend had kept his word and was waiting for her. She would clap her hands with joy and rest her head on her father's shoulders, and then go to sleep. Ah! in after years how the memory of those visits haunted her! How often she wished she could rest her head as in days of old, with no thoughts of the future, and sleep the innocent dreamless sleep of childhood! The girl had not to wait long for her father. In the distance she saw a figure wading through the rice fields, and with alacrity she bounded down and joined the old man. He took her up and put her on his shoulders, and lovingly she slipped her hands round his head and said with a tremulous voice :—" Three days, father, three days I have waited for you and you never came, and it grew dark and the idol stared at me, the owls hooted and I was alone."

" Hush, child! Here we are at home."

The house was a little hut with a neatly swept cowdunged verandah shaded by trees. The *tulsi** grew on a pedestal in the enclosure in front, and there was a well on one side with shining water vessels round it. As the father and child entered, the old woman growled and said :—" I see what the girl has been

* A sacred plant.

about. Ah! you little truant. You knew your father was coming home."

The father smiled, and the girl rubbed her face on his shoulder half hiding it. "Is she a bad child?" said he, affectionately.

"Bad enough," was the rejoinder, "with all your spoiling. Why, she gets more petting than a son would," and the old dame went in to bring them their supper while the father washed himself at the well. The girl waited for her father with a peculiar wistful expression in her eyes, then the plantain leaves were spread, the food was served, and father and child enjoyed their simple meal of *dal bhat*.*

The hillock, or rather the mound, on which the house was situated, formed part of a great sacred hill famed for its pilgrimages. The scenery around was pretty and homely, but just here it was weird and desolate. The little shrine or temple belonging to this particular part—for each hillock had some sort of a shrine of its own—was mostly in ruins. The trees were stunted, the houses were little better than huts built mostly out of the broken ruins of the temple, and the clear tank that had been supplied by mountain springs had overflowed its stony basin and was rolling down the valley, a noisy tumbling stream. The wind, coming in tremendous gusts, shrieked and whistled round the temple and roared in the empty passages. Caught in the trees it shook their branches in terrible confusion, then tore past the bare bleak mountain rocks, and moaned over the tank a sad, sad

* Rice and pulse.

dirge, which mingled with the voice of the stream in weird and mysterious harmony. There was a mountain cave whose pebbly sides showed that in former years it had been the bed of a stream now dried up. Near the cave was the girl's hut, and other huts lay scattered round it with the thick foliaged *neem* trees between. Here the whistling of the winds was the loudest, so that neither by night nor by day could one feel all alone. A road from the city led on to the main hill, the great sacred hill crowded with its temples, its shining domes, its stony passages, and pillared halls. From a distance came borne on the breeze the never-ceasing din of *tom-toms*,* bells, and musical instruments.

The little girl, Kamala, was an only child, and she was devotedly fond of her father. Her mother had died when she was quite young, and her recollections of her mother were very faint. The picture of a fair tall lady with large sad eyes often came to her in dreams, and she remembered a time when she was fondled and petted and called sweet names. But that time seemed very long ago, and only the image of her mother's eyes came before her with any distinctness. Their soft sweet light shone round her in dreams, and sometimes in the starlit evenings they would come back to her. Then she felt the sweet presence of some one near her and in this blessed delusion she would fall asleep.

Kamala's life had hitherto been a very uneventful one. The dawn of each day was ushered in by the

* The Hindu drum.

music of the temple close by, the soft ringing of bells, the long drawn chants of the Brahmans saying their prayers, and the hushed refrain of the *pujaris* who intoned their *mantras** with a peculiar drawl, and the mingled faint din of the waking city below. The song of the birds was dear to the girl, but not so dear as the soft melody of the chants of the Brahmans which, though she understood them not, filled her soul with feelings of devotion. Thus stirred from sleep she hastened to make her own *puja*† to the gods that gave her all the good things of life. She was fond of the Sudra girls who every morning tended the cows and goats that grazed beside her home. From them she received most willing assistance in the many household duties that she had to preform. By them also the little girl had her head filled with superstitions and exaggerated accounts of occurrences that took place in the neighbouring villages. But her father occupied her attention most. It was her duty to fill his *chembu*‡ with water, to lay his plantain leaf ready for food, to water the *tulsi* tree, and to attend to other domestic duties under the direction of the old dame, whom she called granny. The greater part of the day however she spent with her father, who generally sat in the temple verandah which was densely shaded with trees. She would nestle by his side and listen to his learned talk; for he was a recluse and a scholar. Brought up in this way, unlike other girls of her own age, she was shy, retiring and innocent.

* Sacred verses. † Worship. ‡ Brass vessel.

Besides the diversions she had by her occasional visits to the city, one incident in particular served as a break in the life of comparative monotony which she led. This was the festival which was celebrated in honour of the presiding goddess of the temple close by. Early in the morning on the day of the festival a troop of little girls ascended the hillock in their gala attire, accompanied by old dames and widows. It was the festival of *Anjini,* the goddess of wind, which came once in ten years. Pandals were erected round the temple, and all the way down to the city fairy *mantapams** had risen in the night. The temple music was in its glory, and when it ceased the beat of the *tom-tom* was heard all around. The wind strangely enough on that day veered towards the mountain side and blew with more than its usual force. It was a delightful sight to see the usually desolate hillock alive with people all bent on mirth and enjoyment.

The festival being only a local one, was not of very great importance, but it was duly observed by the women folk in the city below, who considered it unpropitious to begin a decade without making offerings to the goddess who presided over wind, rain, and sunshine. The people bathed in the stream and filled their *chembus* with the clear temple water. The girls brought simple offerings of flowers, rice, *kunkun,*† and other things, and went away making silent vows in return for favours asked. There was the religious

* A temporary decorated shed.

† Red lead used in toilet.

mendicant dancing quaintly round the *margosa* tree, blowing on his horn and performing many antics, and getting in return copper coins from the laughing spectators. Near the temple the *bhairagis** and *ghosavis** were prominent, each with a brass plate and some kind of crude musical instrument making as much noise as possible. Inside, in the dark recess of the temple, where the goddess was enshrined, were the *pujaris*, solemn and repulsive, with huge marks on their foreheads. There were also seen men and women silently bowing and prostrating themselves before the goddess. The lights flickered here and there in the dark recess and gave to the whole an air of solemnity.

Near her own hut stood Kamala, shy, not knowing what to do. It was a new experience in her life to see so many people come to the temple which she regarded as her own. She had seen festivals in other places, but at this particular festival she thought she should take a prominent part; for, was not her father the greatest man there and was he not looked up to and revered by all around? She felt possessed of a dignity all her own as she sallied out in her best attire. But the sight of a group of girls of her own age staring at her made her shy, and she would have hid herself had they not gathered round and poured questions on her. They looked at her dress and her jewels and made remarks about her without the slightest respect for her feelings. "Where do you live?" "Where do you come from?" were questions that she

* Different classes of religious mendicants.

heard on all sides. "Surely you are not the *sanyasi's** daughter." "How old are you?" "Why are you not married?" "Have you lived here all your life?" "What a peculiar cloth you have on!"

The little girl was dazed and bewildered at having attracted so much attention. She looked round with tears in her eyes, when an older girl more sympathetic than the rest drew her away, saying to the other girls:—"You are frightening her, don't you see?" and took her aside. Then one of the girls asked:— "Is it true that you are coming down to the city with your father to live there."

"I do not know, father never told me."

"Father! Surely he is not your father, an old man like that," said an elderly dame with a mischievous twinkle in her eyes. "Perhaps he has picked you up somewhere."

At this, Kamala's eyes again filled with tears, and in a trembling but indignant voice she said:—"He *is* my father and no one may say that he is not."

"Where is your mother?"

"Mother! I have none, but I have a grandmother."

"Ha! Ha! Ha!" laughed the giris. "Do you mean to say that the old crone is your grandmother? We can't swallow that. We know her well: she is Ganesh's grandmother."

Kamala, now crest-fallen, looked completely bewildered while the girls jeered as before. Once more the big girl who took her aside, came to her rescue and said:—"Never mind, you don't know. They

* One who has renounced the world.

told you to call her 'grandmamma' but she is not your grandmamma."

"Then she is my mother's grandma," said the girl, turning round brightly and seeing her way out of the difficulty.

At this there was more jeering. But it was soon suppressed; for the tall girl looked round with great displeasure and checked them saying:—"What fools to laugh! Don't you see, she knows nothing." So saying she put her arm round Kamala's neck and asked her in a soft voice where she got the pearls that glistened on her neck, adding, "Don't you know they are real?"

The necklace was the only jewel the girl possessed, and her father allowed her to wear it little thinking of its value.

"Pearls!" said all the girls grasping her necklace. "Oh! Oh! Are they really pearls?"

But Kamala drew herself closer to the big girl, Kashi, and simply said:—"They have been always on me. I think I was born with them, and I play with them." Then turning away from the group of girls round her, she exclaimed:—"See there a father and a mother with their children." She laughed and the girls laughed too, and left her with the tall girl who exacted a promise from Kamala to come and see her in the city. "Tell your father, 'Ramkrishna Punt's daughter is my friend,' and your father will bring you to me. He knows my father." Kamala gazed into Kashi's eyes with such a responsive look of trustful joy that the big girl could not help clasping the little one in her arms.

But soon the temple rounds had to be made. The girls offered flowers to the goddess, drank the holy water, and touched their foreheads with the holy ashes. All these sacred duties they performed with scrupulous care, and Kashi seemed to be the leader of them all. She bought flowers and fastened them in Kamala's hair, and when going, reminded her of her promise.

The sun rose and beat over the hills and plains with a fierce light. The breeze fell and the morning festival came to an end. Kamala retired to her hut to talk over the events of the festival with her father, and to tell him of the new friend who had so cordially invited her to her home.

CHAPTER II.

A group of little girls are seen at a well in the back-yard of Kashinath Punt's house in the city. Their brass pots are laid down on the stony pavement that surrounds the well. There is apparently an animated conversation going on, and the gestures of the girls indicate suppressed excitement. A rippling flow of laughter now and then breaks forth from the girls as they talk in the fulness of youthful spirits. A big girl with a huge vessel on her side joins them, and all hail her eagerly saying, "Come, Come, Bhagirathi! We want you to make up the number seven."

"Are there not seven sisters among the stars, seven daughters of the King? and we are seven now," said one with a side glance and a twinkle in her eyes."

"Seven demons of misfortune, seven plagues, rather," said another, laughing. "Why, Indra himself was afraid of the number seven, and so Arjuna was created to make up the eighth."

"Stop your learned nonsense. You know nothing of Arjuna nor of Varuna," said the *shastri's* daughter.

"I tell you I know all about it," maintained Harni, the one contradicted. "We had the Puranic reading last night at our house and we had such a gathering. By the bye, have you seen the *sanyasi's* daughter Kamala? Ramakrishna Punt's daughter, Kashi, brought her to our house."

"I see Kamala is the great friend now, and Kashi shows off the girl wherever she goes," said another girl, with a smile of disdain and a proud curl on her lip.

"Why! my mother was off her head last night," added Gungi, a short fat girl, with an ill-natured sneer. "The way in which she petted the little minx and put flowers in her hair was most provoking. She kept on saying to us the whole evening that Kamala was so sweet, and had no mother, and so on. I think she would like to play the mother herself."

"Ha! Ha! Ha! To play the mother-in-law rather," laughed the other girls. "You have a brother, haven't you—studying somewhere? just the thing."

"*She* for my brother! Why, I wouldn't tolerate her a day in the house," was Gungi's reply. "Good looks! why, Kamala has no good looks. She looks shy and frightened and stupid as if she had not been brought up among human beings."

"What can you expect of her when her father spends half his time in the jungle?" said Bhagirathi, "I don't wonder that she is like that. My father thinks much of the old man though. Poor man! They say he was very rich once but nobody knows."

"I don't believe a word of it," said Gungi, with a toss of her head. Then lifting her vessel, which was already filled with water, she placed it on her side and returned home. The other girls laughed at this outburst of ill-temper, and then taking up their own vessels they returned home as solemnly as if they had never met before.

* * * *

It is evening—one of those evenings very common in mountainous places, where the sunlight lingers on the tops of the hills loath to depart, while the world around is growing dark. The stars are beginning to peep out from the wide expanse of sky overhead. Kamala is alone among the trees, between whose gnarled trunks she catches glimpses of the western horizon. The brown stones and bare rocks around seem to increase in size mysteriously in the deepening twilight, and the rustling of the trees appears ominous to her superstitious mind. She looks at the deserted scene around her and trembles. To her simple mind each tree has its mysterious occupant, and though naturally brave, she is a little timid on this occasion, as she had never before strayed so far away from home.

"Dada! Dada!" she cried, as she cautiously stepped over the stones and among thorny bushes and peered down as far as she could into the valley before her. A shepherd lad had told her that her father was coming in that direction. There were three visitors at home, one of whom, a woman, had sent her in haste to fetch her father. Everything was growing more and more weird and desolate and she was about to return when the figure of a man suddenly emerged from the dark space below. He had ascended a sharp curve of the hillock, and he seemed surprised when he came suddenly upon her. He looked at her for a moment and then stood still, as if trying to recollect something he had forgotten, and the girl also stood still looking at him waiting for him to speak; but when he did not say anything, she said simply: "I have come to look for my father and it is getting so late. Have you seen him anywere?"

"Your father? Who are you, little girl? I have come here from a distant place gathering herbs, and I saw nobody down there. But don't be frightened. I daresay I know your father; tell me who he is."

"My father is the *sanyasi*; and we both live here."

"Of course I know the *sanyasi* Narayan. Lead me to the place where he lives. I daresay he is there already. Don't be frightened; I am your father's friend."

Kamala said nothing and looked at his face at first with some misgiving, but there was something so reassuring in the strong manly countenance and in the pleasant eyes that looked down on her that she could not help feeling bold. "Come," she said simply, and walked in front while he followed her.

When they reached the hut, her father was already there. She ran to him and said:—"There is somebody asking for you. He is outside. Where are the visitors?" and then added: "I was looking for you, Dada, and could not find you. I was near the lightning struck tree when I saw the person outside."

"You ought not to have gone so far. Yes, I have seen the visitors. But who is this new caller? Let me see." So saying, he rose and went out.

Why did Kamala's father look so bent and aged? And why was there such a change in him immediately after, when he saw the stranger? His face brightened, and the look of joy in his eyes made him appear quite different from what he had been a moment before. The evening light was rapidly vanishing but there was enough to see the face of the stranger, who also seemed to be overjoyed at meeting his friend. The old man grasped the *neem* tree close by and stood for a second looking at the young visitor, and then his countenance fell as he gasped out, "Come at last! Oh! why have you come *now*."

"Hush! don't talk," said the stranger, "let us go yonder amongst the trees. Is that your little daughter?"

"It is too late now. What shall I do?" said the old man to himself in piteous tones, without paying any heed to the words of the stranger.

"Why is it that father is so moved? What can he have done?" Thus questioning herself Kamala came forward and stood by her father's side, but he sent her away with almost a harsh voice, saying, "Go in Kamala! You must not wander out in the evenings alone."

After some time the old man returned home, but the stranger was not with him. Kamala was seated with the old woman near the fire-place, watching intently the operation of cooking, but when her father returned he took her out and they both sat on the raised basement in front of the house. By this time it was night, and the stars shone brightly overhead. The light of the moon glimmered faintly among the trees in front and the voice of the stream was hoarse and loud. Kamala's head rested on the old man's knee and, as he stroked and petted her, he told her his secret. "You are to be married," he said, "and I can't help it. It was arranged some time ago. The visitors came to see you more than me. I have had a great struggle, but it is all over. Your father-in-law to be is a *pundit* well known to me. His wife was here this evening. Are you satisfied, my little girl?" There was a ring of pain in his voice.

The idea of marriage was not unfamiliar to Kamala. She knew she was to be married some day, for the old woman had often said that it was high time she was married, and had grumbled over and over again at the delay, and her father had also sometimes jovially added: "Yes! she is troublesome enough, I shall have to get rid of her soon."

The little girl anticipated the event only thinking of it as a prospective gala day in her life. But now, why did her father speak to her in such an apologetic tone and why did he look so troubled? Why did he say, "I can't help it. I wish it was otherwise. You must go and be like other girls, toil for your own food and be at the mercy of others." Work! What was there new in that? Even now she was brought up to work. Did she not know how to cook food? The little girl's eyes had opened wide with wonder and she looked at her father and said, "Yes, Dada! I know how to work, don't fear."

He tried to avoid her gaze and said, "Don't look like that"—a remark which he had often made whenever she looked searchingly at him, and she wondered still more what there was in her eyes to trouble her father. But he merely patted her and said that she was a good girl and would bring credit to him wherever she went.

The next day preparations were made for the marriage. It was the mother of Gungi—the girl who had so warmly protested against Kamala—that was to be Kamala's mother-in-law. Kashi, whom Kamala visited often, did not like the idea of her friend being married into Gungi's family, and she would have asked her father to use his influence to prevent the marriage, but the matter had been settled already and it was too late to interfere.

The marriage day was approaching, a great day in the life of a little girl, and one which is looked forward to with eagerness. The pageantry and the excitement of the event have a peculiar charm for children, who are of course utterly ignorant of the nature of marriage and look upon it in the light of a festival. So Kamala took all the preparations made for her marriage as a matter of course. The evening before the eventful day came at last. The whole day had been one of great excitement and it was with difficulty that Kamala, who was the centre of attention, got outside the house. No wonder she felt depressed. The continued excitement of the past few days had brought about a reaction, and combined with this was the strange but indistinct misgiving felt in her heart at the change that was about to take place in her life. Her future mother-in-law had called often, and more than once had taken her to task for her carelessness and ignorance. She was comparatively a stranger to Kamala, but the latter having been taken more than once to her future home had had a foretaste of the position she was to occupy in it as a daughter-in-law; and now, though decorated and made much of, she felt a great weariness come over her. She lingered by the temple ruins, and as she gazed on the clear waters of the tank in front, and listened to the voice of the wind and the stream close by and the familiar twittering of the birds, her eyes filled with tears, and, turn where she would, she felt miserable. The little home she was to leave so soon was never so dear as it was then, and even the cross old dame that took care of her seemed to have a new charm about her, and her father,—she felt a choking in her breast at the thought of leaving him. He was a peculiar father. She knew no love but his, and it was no common love that surrounded her. He had been all in all to her from her babyhood,—her nurse, her confidant, and her instructor. Now, poor girl, she knew not what awaited her in the future. She was to go down, she knew, to live among strangers in the city on the other side—the city that seemed so dreadfully large and unfriendly to her; and with these thoughts she sat down on a stone close by. But she was not left long by herself. Little children came running up to her in great excitement crying out to her: "Kamala! Kamala! you are needed inside." The jewels had to be tried on and the goldsmith was waiting to put the finishing touch to them. The flowers had already come. "Such heaps of them," said the eager voices. "And, Kamala, what a lot of people are gathering—why, the *pandal* in front and the two sheds round the house, all are full!"

"And the cooking," said one, "heaps of cakes and sweet things are being made at the back, I just had a peep at them. And rice is coming in sacks. Yeshi's villagers, Dashrath's headman, and the old shepherd—all have brought *dal*, rice, ghee, any amount." "Come, come, there is no end of fun. The *tom-tom* is going to beat and it will beat for *three* days running."

In the meantime another batch had rushed out and taken their turn in giving other breathless messages. Kamala caught the excitement and laughed loudly. She took the hands of two little ones and was going to run in when she saw Kashi and her mother and two other girls coming up from the path below towards the house. The girls as soon as they caught sight of Kamala, called out to her: "Come along! come along! what are you doing there. The bride is actually hiding herself. See what we have brought for you."

Kamala ran out to meet them, and at the sight of Kashi's venerable mother she drew back, covered her head, and, with a shy respectful look, bowed herself at the old lady's feet,—a common way of making obeisance to older women or to people of higher rank. "Get up little girl. Don't be so shy," said the old lady, and patted her while the girls laughingly besmeared Kamala's face and hands with sandal-wood powder made into a paste, which they had brought in silver vessels. "Enough! Enough!" said the old lady, "there is time enough to do all that to-morrow. Come along," and they all entered Kamala's house. As they did so all the women assembled made their respectful obeisance to Kashi's mother, for she was the wife of a great man, the *mamlatdar** of Sivagunga. They took her to the seat of honour, where a long pillow was placed on a huge rug spread at the further end of the *pandal,* which was screened for the women.

"It is indeed an honour to have you here on this occasion," said Gungi's mother.

"Oh! it is nothing. Kamala is like my own daughter We are all so fond of her, and I wasn't going to let her get married without my being present. See this is Kashi's present to her." So saying she took out a little necklace and gave it to Gungi's mother.

"This is very kind indeed. Come along Kamala, and fall at this lady's feet and show proper gratitude, child. Kashibai, you will make Kamala quite proud."

Kamala came forward and bowed her head and sat by the old lady. There was something so sad in her gaze and humble obeisance that the old lady drew Kamala towards her and said:—"Poor girl, your mother, what would she not have done for you if she had been living?" and lifting the girl's drooping head, added: "Let me put it on you."

While some other jewels were being tried on the bride her pearls attracted the attention of the old lady, who said, "Her mother must have been very rich. Poor people don't put pearls on their daughters. I wonder where the other jewels are."

"The father is so peculiar; one doesn't know what to make of him," said one of the guests present.

* A Revenue officer.

"And much he knows about jewels," added the grumbling old woman who took care of Kamala, "why, he does not know gold from brass. I never saw a man so careless or indifferent about money. No wonder he took to such a life. He lets Kamala grow up like a boy, and the girl is no better than the father. She will tell you the contents of many books though, picked up, you know, from her father." And all looked at Kamala and laughed.

The men sat in the outer half of the *pandal* in front, with trays of sweets and betel leaves in their midst. Kamala's father was there also, but he kept himself in the background, for, as a *sanyasi*, he was not expected to take any part in the receiving or entertaining of guests. The distinguished visitors, however, sought his company, and conversed with him. A change came over the recluse. His bent head was raised, and his thoughtful face with its deep forehead and dark keen eyes, wore its wonted expression of dignity.

CHAPTER III.

THE whole night was spent in preparing for the festivities of the morrow. People gathered from all sides. There were the friends and relatives of the bridegroom's party; there were the *sanyasi's* special acquaintances, the *shastris* and *pundits* of the city below, with their families, and the *pujaris* of the temple close by; and there was also a large number of Sudras who had come to assist in the outside work. Kamala had the special satisfaction of seeing her favourite Sudra friend, Yeshi, and her whole family there, making themselves useful in various ways. She had known them from her childhood. They seemed to be part of the woods, the hills, and the glens around her. She used to hear their voices in the woods singing to themselves a loud hearty melody while the sound of their axes echoed and re-echoed in the glens below. It was from their loud conversations as they went about doing their work that she gathered her knowledge of the wide world; and when the fields below, those long undulating stretches of green, were ripening in the sun, the girl used to watch with deepening interest the operations of reaping, thrashing, and gathering; and would try to recognize among the workers her own special friends, Yeshi and her brothers. Their old father was a favourite also. He did no work, though in the evening he demanded the best of food. It was the duty of Yeshi's mother to get him his *curry* in the evenings, and when it was not forthcoming she received a beating from him, which, however, she took in a very cool matter-of-fact way. Sometimes Yeshi's face also would swell up suspiciously, and when asked the reason, she would answer, with a broad smile, "Oh! It is nothing. Father did not get his *curry* and I had a share in mother's beating," and then she would naively add, with her hand lifted to her face, "Does it look very bad?" and would laugh heartily over it. Simple people! they had their own peculiar traits, good and bad, but they were faithful, honest, and, as a rule hard-working, and would do anything for those who were kind to them.

The morning of the marriage was one of those mornings common in the month of September—cold and crisp. The rays of the sun shone aslant the hills and the dewy leaves glistened and rustled in the fresh cool breeze. The red leaved *thworna* bushes mingling with the *neem* and the tender wavy shoots of the bamboo, with here and there a gigantic *pallus* towering overhead, its autumnal leaves all red and yellow, made a pretty picture, and Kamala, as she looked down into the valley arrayed in its fresh morning garb, was tempted to go down in spite of her grandmother's orders. She stepped over the cool dew-washed stones, picking here and there a wild flower which she pressed against her cheek, and with each gust of wind she felt the happy buoyancy of life which made her forget that she was a bride. The song of the birds rang out sweet and clear. *Tew Tew* rose to the heavens, and filled the whole valley; and Kamala felt the melody dance in her veins, and in her wild delight she too danced round the trees with *Tew, Tew, Whew, Whew* on her lips. It was very early, and the servants and guests, who had remained up late the night before were still asleep, when Kamala left the house; so she felt free to do what she liked. She ran and jumped over the stones like a mountain goat, and sang out in her joy whatever came to her lips.

All this time she was being observed by a person who stood behind a tree. It was an unexpected sight to see the bride of the previous evening, who was almost too shy to lift her head, so completely given up to the enjoyment of life as Kamala then was; and the picture impressed itself indelibly on the mind of her observer, who was no other than her father-in-law. It enabled him better to understand the girl's character, and he was pleased and greeted her with a kindly smile. Her first glance at the intruder was one of surprise. When she recognised who he was she felt a throb of shame and fear. "Had she done wrong in dancing and singing? What would others say if they knew it?" and the mocking, jeering faces of the girls came before her. She therefore put her head down and moved aside, and would have run away had her father-in-law not spoken to her in a kindly tone

"Stop! stop! girl. Dont't run away. I see this is your morning occupation." Kamala had never before met him alone, but always in the company of others, where he appeared grave, stern, and unapproachable, but now when she saw his smiling face she became sufficiently bold to talk to him. "I ought not to be here," she said. "Granny told me not to go very far, but I was running and didn't know."

At this he laughed and said, "Never mind, little girl, go inside." The laugh sounded kindly in her ears and she felt somehow that she had a friend in him.

Kamala had to go through several ceremonies that day, but the most important were at night when she had to sit by the side of the bridegroom on a flat stool, with brass lamps all ablaze around, facing the holy fire in front. The *mantras* repeated by the Brahmans were unintelligible to both. The only persons close to them were the mother-in-law and the father-in-law, and, at the auspicious moment the *Brahmagath*, the silken knot, never to be untied, which united them for life, was tied. Living or dead she was henceforth the wife and the property of the man whoever he might be. This was ordered by the *shastras*, and the law was never to be broken. There was one more interesting ceremony to be gone through that night. It was when the bride and bridegroom went out in the moonlight and scanned the heavens to find out the moon's companion, the tiny star *Rohini*, the discovery of which is regarded as conferring life-long companionship and happiness on a young couple.

The bride and bridegroom were the subjects of a great deal of fun and laughter. The incident which caused the greatest merriment was their attempts to use each other's names in rhymed couplets—a common custom at a Hindu marriage. They were prevented from sitting down to dinner by damsels who gathered round them. The bridegroom was the first to be pounced upon.

"Take the name of your wife. The guests are waiting for their dinner," said they.

The young man, who had no alternative, made ridiculous efforts at rhyming. Every failure was hailed with a burst of laughter, and jokes were cracked at his expense. "Oh! he is quite ashamed of her," remarked the matrons. "If he does not know how to rhyme his wife's name with a good word he had better not have her."

After much teasing he at last succeeded in making the following awkward couplet: "Stars, stars in pearls, and the best in flowers is Kamala my wife."

At this there was a fresh burst of laughter. "Who ever saw stars in pearls? and the best in flowers is a rose and not your Kamala,* you conceited youngster," said an old woman.

A flush of shame came over Kamala's face and she looked at her husband with a shy side glance to see how he took the rebuke. Her turn, too, came soon, and her trial was harder still. She was at a loss to know how to get a rhyme containing that most unpoetical of names Ganesh,† the name of her husband. Prompted, however, by the matrons she said: "Paraded is the big-bellied god once a year, but my husband Ganesh mounts the elephant's *ambari* every day."

* Kamala is the lotus.

† Ganesh is the name of the big-bellied god.

She thought that she had successfully passed through the ordeal not knowing that she had added her husband's name unconsciously just as he had taken hers, and to her surprise she saw shocked faces all round her, and loud hisses and laughter came from all sides.

"*Hari! Hari!*" they exclaimed in unison. "Break cocoanuts. Break cocoanuts! She will be the most undutiful wife. She has taken her husband's name!"

"Don't you know, you little stupid," said an old woman shaking her, "that a husband's name is to be heard, but never pronounced by a wife. He can take your name, but you can't take his. Make your *Prayaschita* now." Thus ended the farce.

The next three days were days of intense excitement, during which the festivities were kept up with great spirit. After these were over, Kamala was carried triumphantly in a procession to her husband's home. Before going down to the city, her father had called her aside and told her that he was not going with her, but if she wanted him she had simply to send word to him; and, taking her once more in his arms, he kissed her. She clung to his neck and said: "Oh! why are you not coming?"

"You must try to do without me, child, hereafter," he said, with a choking voice.

There was nobody there to witness this parting scene. The girl herself did not realize what the parting really meant till she went to her husband's home. There she knew her loss and in vain longed for her loved Dada who was all in all to her.

The Brahman quarter of the city of Sivagunga,

which consists of a single long, winding street, is packed mostly with low thick-walled houses, each with a shaded verandah in front. Here and there, there are a few larger houses projecting in front, some one-storied, and some with two stories. These houses extend at the back to the bank of the river, and each has a private bathing-place of its own, the *ghauts*, the common bathing-place, being further on. On the *pials** are seen fair Brahman childern scantily clad, with their characteristic jewels and their hair either tied in top-knots or hanging in low plaits behind. In front, the houses look insignificant and small; but behind each opens out into a court-yard with out-houses and a small garden. The houses communicate with each other by means of paths leading through the hedges, and the women while at work often keep up a running conversation with their neighbours. The wells in the backyards are usually scenes of great bustle, and around a well with exceptionally good water there gather groups of girls and women who have come from far and near with brass pots and other water vessels.

It was early morning. Men and women returning from the river with wet clothes and *chembus* full of water, hastened hither and thither in all directions. The air resounded with a busy din. On all sides were heard the cries: Bhagighya Bhagi!† Dahighya Dahi.‡ The fruit-sellers also lauded their goods in

* Raised platforms constructed of stone in front of the house.

† Buy, Buy vegetables!

‡ Buy, Buy curds.

cheerful, vociferous tones, indulging now and then in amusing extemporised rhymes.

"Halloa! What brings you here?" said a tall man with a big-built frame and a commanding countenance in which sternness and reserve were mingled with the proud Brahmanical features. He was standing in the verandah of one of the larger houses in the street and was accosting a Sudra who had taken off his shoes and was respectfully coming forward to hand a letter. The Brahman received the letter with a "hump" and went inside. The letter-carrier's betel-nut bag was out in an instant; and taking the betel leaves in one hand and a lump of *chunam** in the other he sat down to mix the ingredients, and with a self-satisfied look in his face grinned at the woman who came with a basket of pails on her head to milk the cows and also at the vegetable-seller just then entering the backyard by the side door. He also cracked jokes with the gardener who was digging ostentatiously beneath the few *mogra* trees that grew in tufts by the side of the house.

"There is more pleasure in the air and more *bakshish*,† for the young man is coming down soon," said the letter-carrier.

"What, passed?"

"Yes! *passed* right away," said the other with a look of conscious knowledge, and that air of importance usually assumed by servants when they use English words.

At that moment a country cart stopped in front

* Calcium hydrate. † Money.

and then all was astir. The driver shouted out as he drew up: "Ram! Ram! Gopala! Baisahib is come."

The gardener jumped up and ran to the cart and lifted out three half-naked childern and then helped to bring out a number of bundles of all sizes, while the people in the house rushed to the door.

"Who is come? Who is come? Is Ramabai come?" ran the cry, and an elderly dame, who was no other than Kamala's mother-in-law, stepped out and the half-naked childern ran to her. She took them and kissed them, and seeing a man get down from the cart, she covered her head and asked if all was well. When all the bundles were removed, Ramabai alighted and was caressed by her mother, for it was the elder daughter and her husband who had arrived. In the verandah Ramabai looking respectfully down and answering her father's question, said:—"We had a nice journey."

"That is well. That is well," said the old man. "Go inside and rest yourself. You need rest. Did you halt at the Shepherd's Inn by the way?"

"No, we came straight on."

"That is well too, for there are rumours of robbers on the road." By this time Ramabai's husband, having got all the bundles inside the house, came forward to greet his father-in-law. He was a short, stout man, with irregular features, and rather dark for a Brahman. Ramabai made haste to hug her sister Gungi who had just come out with a smile on her dark fat face. A slim fair girl stood far in the background, near the inner quadrangle of the house.

She did not come forward but merely bent her head down at the approach of Ramabai.

"Oh! Is this Kamala?" said Ramabai gathering her *saree** and passing on with a look of undisguised contempt to the side-room to which the bundles had been taken. The three children, however, stood around Kamala and stared at her very hard. Kamala, not knowing what to do, passed in also to the side-room where the bundles lay, and as she entered she heard Gungi say rather loudly: "Shut up those things and don't take them out now," for Ramabai was untying some of the bundles. The mother was also there and all sat and talked excitedly while Kamala stood near the door of the adjoining room and looked on.

---

* The upper cloth worn by Hindu females.

CHAPTER IV.

IT was now six months since Kamala had come to her husband's house. Her first experiences were happy. Gungi disliked her, but both her father-in-law and her mother-in-law treated her kindly. Gungi, finding that Kamala was superior to her in many respects, felt herself thrust in the background, and this she could not forgive. What was there about Kamala that won people's hearts? Her eyes appealed to one even when she was spoken to roughly, and she moved about with a pose of the head and an air that marked her out as distinctly superior to those around her. For a time Gungi was baffled by her soft sweet ways and her willingness to do every duty that was laid upon her. The heaviest drudgery was light in her eyes, for she was doing it for her own father. He would know that she did not shrink from anything. The old man, her father-in-law, resembled her own father very much, for he was a *shastri* also, and like him fond of the same musty old books. He would pat her when she looked eagerly into his face as she had done into her father's; and the little girl, feeling the loss of her own father, drew near to the old man. He used to wonder at first at her little attentions to him, her guileless ways, and her total ignorance of the relationship he bore to her as a father-in-law, a man more to be feared than loved. When he was in his study, a front room set apart for him into which no one dare go, she would fearlessly go to him after her work was over and stay there quietly arranging his books for him or watching him with a mute love while he was deep in study. At first he felt uncomfortable at the little stranger's taking to him so, but after some time he got accustomed to it and even looked out for her coming. She appeared somehow to help him in his studies, and one day he discovered to his great surprise that she knew what was inside the books, for once when arranging and dusting them she said very naively: "Shall I keep the book with the *shlokas** of creation on the top? Shall you require it to-day?"

"What do you know of the *shlokas* of creation?" he asked, turning round sharply on her. She was frightened at first, but replied innocently with an upward glance: "I know them. My father was very fond of them. I think I understand them."

Oh! those dark large eyes! what a world of innocence, love, and trust they expressed! He felt the look go through him and said gently: "You understand? Tell me, are you able to read?"

"Very little," she said with a sigh, "but father used to repeat the *shlokas* so often that I knew them all long ago, when I used to lie in his arms and be lulled to sleep by them."

"And who taught you to read?"

"I don't know how I learnt. I used to play at learning to read on the sand when I was small, and father used to put me right and say that it was right

* Sacred verses.

that the daughter of a reading man should know how to read. He would add: 'Lakshmi could read.'"

"And who was Lakshmi?" said her father-in-law.

"She must have been my second self, for he called me Lakshmi at times, and spoke of her as one who lived long ago. I used to say she was my shadow, for there was Kamala in front and Lakshmi her shadow behind. Isn't that funny?" And she laughed and hid her face, while he stroked her head and wondered at her innocence.

Now it was against all rules of decorum for a daughter-in-law to be so very familiar with her father-in-law, and to be in such favour with him. Gungi found cause to misinterpret this dreadfully. She assigned all kinds of wicked motives to Kamala, saying that she despised the company of herself and her mother, she was immodest and bold, and that the air of humility which she put on was but a mask to conceal her boldness. She worked well, Gungi said, in order that she might have more time to be in the company of her father-in-law, and influence him against his own daughter. At first these complaints were not listened to by Gungi's mother, who petted Kamala and said: "Let her get as much love as she can. Poor girl! she has no father."

Gungi's mother was a simple impressionable sort of woman, very easily led by others, and under the excitement of the moment expressed her feelings in rather strong language. Hence, prevailed upon by the continued complaints of Gungi, she covertly scolded the old man for what she considered his callous indifference to the family, now and then throwing out hints against Kamala. "Don't you see how common Gungi looks beside Kamala? Yet you don't make any efforts to get her married. Her jewels and clothes are so ordinary, and you are all for your daughter-in-law. She will of course be in the house. I am tired of hearing people say:—'Oh see what a good daughter-in-law you have. How pretty she is! Where did you get her?' But they take no notice of my girl. If our son also takes to her as you do, why, she will wean away his heart from us and where shall we be? He won't take the least notice of us. Oh! wretched was the day she set foot in this house. The relations murmur, Gungi feels slighted." Thus she tried to poison the old man's mind. He gave up taking Kamala with him to the temple—a distinction conferred on none of the other members of the family. Every action of Kamala's was looked upon by the people in the house with suspicion, and her father-in-law himself began to be indifferent towards her. Gungi triumphed and Kamala pined and shed silent tears, and often hid herself in corners and out-of-the-way places. What could she do? People did not like her. She had done something wrong, something to displease the old man, for when she now and then ran to him with joy he would set her aside and give her some work to do. She would cast furtive glances at him and try to talk; but he would say: "Girls ought to keep silence when elders are busy." This was a mild check but it suppressed the flow of innocent spirits, and damped the joy that arose in her heart.

Her husband she scarcely knew. He left immediately after the marriage ceremony and went to a city not far away for the purpose of study. He was expected to return when he had passed all his examinations. She had a faint recollection of a young man who was made to sit beside her during the marriage ceremonies and feasts, when she had felt most awkward and flurried and had tried to run away. She knew that he was her husband and that by the ceremony and *tamasha* * they had been bound together in some unknown, mysterious way, but she never thought of him or cared to see him again. The outside world began to engage her attention more and more. She began to make the acquaintance of girls of her own age, and their talk revealed a new and dreadful world to her. Her life was no more the life of her childhood. The sweet innocent freedom that belonged to it seemed to have vanished. She learnt many a thing that horrified her. Her eyes would dilate with fear and wonder, and she grew more reserved and quiet.

Kamala's special friends were four in number. They came from neighbouring houses and she frequently met them by the well. At first they avoided the stranger who had come in their midst, and who was seen going about bedecked as a bride. They were jealous, but her frank innocent ways won them. One day they chid her good humouredly for having won the hearts of her mother-in-law and her father-in-law, a thing that was never known before in a Brahman family. "You turn them round your fin-

* Entertainment.

gers," they said. "We hear that 'the syrupy sugar is running in streams in your house.' How did you manage it, you with no father and no mother? Why, you must be a little witch!"

"I have done nothing of the kind," Kamala said, and added with tears: "It is not as you say."

"Yes, we know it won't be very long before you will be brought down from your pedestal. You have such an affectionate sister-in-law!"

"But that is not it," remonstrated Kamala, and was going to explain herself when Bhagirathi, a tall, dark girl, the oldest of them, stopped her, saying: "Yes, yes, we know everything. We have gone through it all ourselves. Only we are astonished at your foolishness and your belief in them. Why, child, don't look so distressed, we each have our troubles at home and the mothers-in-law and the sisters-in-law are not so sweet and innocent as you imagine. A time will come when not a day will pass without your getting a good beating from them or from your husband, and they will try to poison your very food for you. Don't look so blank with wonder. Did not your mother tell you all this? But you had no mother. Poor child! You don't look as if you would stand much beating."

"But we have all to go through it, and you must not be frightened. It is a woman's lot," added Rukhma, the *shastri's* daughter.

"But why will they beat me?"

"For your misconduct, of course. It is always misconduct. If the *ghee* is spilt and you are near it, it must be you, though it was your sister-in-law that did it. You are the evil influence."

"Why, last night I had a beating," said Harni, a soft, fair looking chit of twelve, with tears in her eyes, "because my husband did not take his food. My mother-in-law said that it was I, and though I cried and said I was innocent in the matter, they beat and starved me too."

"That is nothing," said Bhagirathi. "Wait till you get older. You will have enough to suffer from your husband's behaviour. Did you hear of Seeta in the opposite street? Poor girl! Her husband wanted some of her jewels which his own mother had just put on her, and when she would not give them he actually brought a dancing girl to the house and would not send her away till poor Seeta had parted with some of her jewels."

Hearing this Kamala unconsciously put her hand to her necklace, and they all burst out laughing.

"No, not such a jewel as that. Why, it is a mere baby's toy. Your husband won't care for that," said Rukhma.

"But I will give it to him if he wants it," said Kamala in an earnest tone, "and he won't beat me then."

Bhagirathi, moved at her innocence, drew Kamala near to her and said: "No, child! Nobody will beat you. I will see who will. We ought not to tell you all this. 'Whom the gods have not enlightened why should man?' You go in and do everything that they tell you and don't think anybody will beat you."

"What a little simpleton!" said Bheema, a big fat bouncing girl, who all this time was silently looking on. Coming near to Kamala she said: "I will be your friend."

"And I will, too," added fair little Harni, and the four drew near Kamala by the well and their hands met in a solemn compact while Kamala with tears in her glistening eyes looked into their faces.

Kamala's father-in-law, in spite of all the influences brought to bear upon him, had a tender spot in his heart for the little girl. His indifference was only assumed. He was a man of a determined will and once he made up his mind to believe anything it was hard to move him. He felt instinctively that his daughter-in-law was very different from the other girls, and considered himself her special guardian. The scene of the morning of her marriage day, when he found her enjoying nature and revelling in its freedom so unlike other girls, was fresh in his memory, and he could not think that she was capable of deceit of any kind whatever her other qualities might be. In deference to the wishes of his wife, however, he had prevented Kamala from coming often to his study. But from the day of her arrival he had let her pour water on his hands for washing before he took his meals, and had even made her sit near him while he was being served. She took a special delight in sitting near him, and, though other things had changed, this custom was allowed to remain. But the very day her sister-in-law Ramabai came, she ordered Kamala to go and stand inside; and when the old man missed her and inquired for her, Ramabai officiously came forward and said: "Oh, she sits with us women afterwards," for the girls were afraid of the father and did not like him to think that they were unkind to his daughter-in-law. "See to her," he said, "she eats very little, poor child." He even called out to her, but she had been given some work to do just then. After that Kamala never saw her father-in-law during meals.

One evening both the sisters were very grandly dressed, for they were going out to witness a ceremonial to which the whole family had been invited. "Take Kamala, too," said their mother, to which the sisters replied that as Kamala knew nobody it was no use taking her. They asked permission of their mother, however, to let them wear some of Kamala's jewels; and so Kamala was divested of them all—even the pearl necklace and earrings, her father's gifts, which Gungi wore. Then the sisters both went out. Immediately afterwards Kashi entered. Kamala was feeling wretched, but when she saw Kashi her face brightened and she ran to her. But Kashi with a look of anger held her back.

"Who told you to make such a fool of yourself and give away all your jewels to that brat to wear? I just saw her outside. I cannot take you now. I came all this distance to take you to the ceremonial at Ramchandrapunt's house. It is a grand affair and all the world is to be there except of course the old, the lame, the deaf, and the widows. But, my Kamala! What mean those tears and that starved face of yours? Are you not happy?"

"Oh! I don't want to go anywhere. Only you stay near me a little while, and I shall be satisfied. I was feeling so miserable, and I don't know why. I know nobody and I ought not to go. I never felt like this before. I wish I was in my old home far away."

"The truth is, nobody loves you, and there is something wrong somewhere, but come, I must not waste time. You wear this and this," taking off two necklaces from her own neck—"and there you look all right. We must make haste now. How well you look with even those few jewels. We shall baffle them yet."

"But my mother-in-law?"

"I got her permission long ago, and she told me to take you." Kamala, her eyes sparkling with delight, followed her friend to the gathering, and forgetting all her sorrow, spent a happy evening with Kashi.

After Ramabai's return there was a great deal of stir in the house. She rushed up and down, and talked with eager excitement to everybody. She would often take her mother into a room and there form all kinds of plans. Her husband followed her, suggested, discussed, argued, and did as much talking as Ramabai herself. Ramabai's husband had not approved of the marriage, for he seemed to have had some plan of his own. He was disappointed at the turn affairs had taken and found fault with the whole thing. He prided himself on his shrewdness and was ready with interpretations of Kamala's conduct and behaviour which were anything but favourable to her. "What! an only son, the heir to so well known a man to be married to a penniless man's daughter, the antecedents of her mother all unknown and the father none else than a wandering mendicant. What a degradation! Where was the hurry? I fully thought you would wait a year or two more. Able to read and write! A woman cleverer than her husband! This is what the world is coming to. She has already usurped the best place and when the son comes we don't know what tricks she will be up to." He spoke, too, of the great loss that the family had suffered in not getting the son married to the girl he had recommended.

"She is a big man's daughter," he said, "the very alliance would have given your son a lift," and then added: "Even now, well, I don't know what to say, the difficulty is so great." He also spoke in ambiguous terms about some plan he had in view, and threw out certain hints about a young man to whom Kamala had been promised in marriage and who was very much disappointed at not getting her.

Kamala did not understand the reason of all this excitement, nor why they held such hot discussions. Her father-in-law did not join them, and in fact when he was seen to approach there was a calm and hush as if they were afraid of him, though even in his presence Ramabai hurled her stinging remarks at persons and things. Kamala admired the spirit and energy of the woman, but wondered why she herself was so ignored. When in her ignorance she happened to approach the excited party a blight seemed to fall upon them and all eyes were turned on her. Her walk and appearance were marked minutely, and feeling uncomfortable in their presence she would take herself away to some quiet corner. She did not know that she was the subject of a great deal of their excited conversation, neither was she aware that it was partly owing to her husband having passed his examinations and secured an appointment under Government.

CHAPTER V.

IT was night. Hills rose above hills in sullen, silent majesty, piercing the skies. The silver light of the moon fell over all, enhancing the loveliness and solitude of the scene. The fairy veil was brightest over the vast wilderness of peaks as they rose behind one another, dazzling the eye like so many snow-clad mountains. There was a unique grandeur about it all. Nearer, the shimmering light covered in sombre glory the thickly foliaged plants, the mighty forests below, and the wooded sides of the hills, that hid with a soft feathery veil the deep caverns and the dark repulsive ravines. Here and there the moonbeams touched with a tender kiss a solitary bush or a gigantic tree overhanging a precipice. The waters from the neighbouring hills and mountains, sparkling in the light of the moon, like molten silver, dashed down the ravines with a roar, to get lost in the densely wooded valleys below. In the midst of this scene was a table-land containing a few *mutts*, the abodes of religious recluses, who went thither from time to time for prayer and meditation. On this particular night two men were seen on this table-land engaged in earnest conversation. One of these was Kamala's father. The tall thin figure, the peculiar bend of head and walk, and the absent look on the face were unmistakably those of Narayen, the *sanyasi,* the man who lived in himself and in his dreams. What was it that led him to spend half his life in these weird mountain solitudes? What was it that he found so congenial to his cultivated mind in this life of meditation? What was his early history? And why was he unlike other recluses that he did not care for money and gifts offered to him? The person with him was no other than the unexpected young friend who visited Narayen on the eve of Kamala's betrothal.

"Ramchander," said Narayen, "I am sorry for you and for myself. But it is too late, and you will promise me not to see Kamala now. The secret, I hope, is safe in your possession. Happiness does not depend on riches, and I expect my Kamala to be happy as she is. I know from my own experience that when I left the world I was happy till the envious gods and Yama, the enemy of life, deprived me of my wife. Oh! how I should like to have had you as my son, but the fates were against it. I seem to have lost everything with that one great wrench. Kamala alone is left, but I dare not see her, for I should long to have her with me again and she must do without me. Strange that I should find you on the eve of her betrothal. Say, can I rely on you for everything?"

"You may," said the young man, with evident emotion. "I leave Sivagunga to-morrow, but I have left those behind who will watch over your daughter and let you know everything even in these mountain solitudes. May you find the happiness that has eluded you so long. I am off." The young man's face indicated sadness and great disappointment.

* * * * *

The town of Rampur, where Ganesh, Kamala's husband, had gone for study, was not far from Sivagunga. It had an important institution and students from all parts resorted thither for their education. They lived in different parts of the town in bands of three or four, the cheapest and most convenient spot being near the bazaars. Let us dwell for a moment on the sights and sounds familiar to those who live in a narrow street in a crowded part of a town like Rampur. Vegetable and fruit sellers are seen squatted in different parts vending their goods. On one side of the street is a row of sweetmeat shops. In the distance the ironmonger's din and the jingle of the brass vessels is heard, while now and then the uproar is greatest close by, for either a sack of corn has fallen from the overladen carts or a fight is taking place between two cartmen whose carts have got jammed together, and who with their fists are discussing the truth of the doctrine 'might is right.' The people are shouting: "Arrai! Arrai! (Enough! Enough!) *you* go first and *he* goes afterwards." The shopkeepers, stout and greasy looking, scarcely able to move about, stare with indifference, chewing betelnut. The road is stone paved and uneven, and the noise made by the carts is deafening. Here and there are seen groups of Brahmans with their characteristic red shoes, their flowing *dhoties*,* and their

* The upper cloth worn by men.

turbans about the size of a small umbrella. Some have the upper cloth thrown round their necks, others not so well dressed have only a waist cloth and the sacred thread hanging from the shoulders and reaching to the waist.

Overlooking such a busy scene was a dark, upper-storied house, with small, dingy, crudely railed windows. It was occupied by three young men whose ages ranged between eighteen and twenty-four. Two were deep in their books, sitting on ricketty chairs with their legs stretched on a table in front. The third was lounging near the window on a thick heavy mattress, with a long round pillow under his head. A newspaper was in his hand but he laid it down and looked lazily out at the window. After some time one of the two sitting near the table threw his book down and got up with an air of disgust, saying :—
"This is stupid stuff. Ah, Ganesh! You are enjoying your rest. I wish I were in your position. Secured a good place, too, in the Collector's office so soon after passing, and now going home for the holidays."

At this Ganesh looked at the speaker with a smile, yawned lazily, and stretching himself, said: "That dramatic performance which we witnessed last night has undone me. I never felt so tired even after an examination.

"Yes! We know what the attraction was. Take care, Ganesh!"

"I know how to take care of myself. You needn't be alarmed. I was only admiring her wit and beauty from a distance. What a fund of humour she has, and how self-possessed she is, to be sure! She was holding a conversation and actually kept three engrossed near her. I don't think she noticed me. I was far off, but by the gods I could not take myself away from the place."

"She not notice people? She sees them with the corners of her eyes and when she has a hold on them she never leaves them. She is a woman who in olden times would have made kingdoms to rise and fall: she is not like other women."

"No, that is the difference, and therein lies her power over men," said Ganesh. "She is wonderful indeed. Do you know I have heard that she has bands of Bhils who work as her slaves and she is very lavish in her gifts? It looks suspicious, but she seems to know something about every man that others don't know."

"A very dangerous character indeed," added the third young man, who had put down his book and joined in the conversation. "The whole world knows *Sai*. I should like to study her character."

"A very worthy occupation, but wait till you have passed your examination like Ganesh, and then you can take to the study of people's characters," said the other. "Now that you are going home, Ganesh, that is good."

"Yes! and there is no fear of my being influenced by her."

"We shall see! We shall see," said the other students as they left the room for their baths, for it was dinner time.

Ganesh was come of a learned family. His father and his grandfather were *shastris*, noted for their learning and their bigotry. But in these days Sanskrit learning is not appreciated, and those old days have gone when young men of high descent congregated in groves and temples and sat at the feet of learned *shastris* and *pandits*, wearing the mendicant's garb, begging their meals and spending their days in chanting hymns to the gods. The groves are no more the resort of the wise and the good. Sanskrit learning is despised and English learning is all in all, for it pays best. So much against his will the old *shastri* of Sivagunga sent his only son Ganesh to an English school. The old man in his inmost heart had the greatest contempt for English learning, which he regarded as not only superficial but also as antagonistic to the Hindu religion. But he was forced to yield to the influences of the times, and he felt no doubt some satisfaction at the success of his son, though he had his own misgivings as to the influence the new training would have on the young man's religious belief and conduct.

* * * * * *

It was evening in Sivagunga. The streets were unusually quiet, the only sounds heard being the heavy rumbling now and then of a cart or the song of the cartman as he lazily drove his bullocks. The light was fast fading and the narrow streets and shaded places looked dark and dismal. Only in the open spaces near the river did the departing light linger for a little. Groups of girls played in the backyards of their houses. Most of the men had sallied out either to the river-banks for a stroll, or to the bazaars, the general rendezvous of the gossips of the city. The women also, dressed in their best, had left their houses on some pretext or other, either of washing clothes, bringing in water, or making *poojah* to the gods. Kamala was left in the house with only the servant woman who was attending to the cows just come in from their pasture. Her heart was sad. She had of late undergone much hard discipline and she felt as if there was no love left in the world for her poor little self. Nobody cared for her. Her father had not even once come to see her. She felt desolate, and wondered how long all this was going to last. She had tried her best to get into the good graces of Ramabai, who was all-in-all in the house, but it was no use. The woman who seemed so full of spirit, bright and happy, had no kind word for the shy girl who did her best to win the love of her sister-in-law. Kamala would hasten to bring the little things which Ramabai wanted when cooking, or making cakes and other delicacies, at which she was an adept. But no amount of willing labour was of any use. To such questions as:—"Shall I do this?" "May I do the pounding or the rolling, or the kneading?" timidly asked with an eager trembling voice Kamala received but an unwilling grunt of assent, and she looked in vain for a smile of approval while her little hands pounded the dough or rolled out the flat cakes. This particular evening she was seated in a corner of the backyard near a clump of trees overlooking the river. She was giving rein to her thoughts, and the sadness gradually left her as in imagination she beheld her own mountain home, Yeshi and her other friends; and somehow the thought of the fields, the rocks, and the flowers brought quietness and peace to her and filled her heart with a calm joy. She began to think of happy things that were possible even now. "Ramabai will be won over soon. Surely she will love me when she sees how I long for her love. And Gungi will become my friend, and then there will be such happiness," thought Kamala; and she conjured up in her mind visions of going to *Yattras** and festivals with her companions in gala attire, her father with them, and herself happy in the love of all. She even thought of her husband, but was puzzled whether to regard him as her friend or not. She had sat long thinking thus when she heard voices near and trusted that her people had returned. She was preparing to go in when some words fell on her ears that sent a pang through her. She was stunned and her visions fled completely. It was Ramabai who was saying in a tone of disgust in answer to her husband:—................................"Who knows who her mother was? That she, a penniless girl, should be thrust on us in this way. My poor father, how he was taken in! Now there is this golden opportunity. What a grand match it would have been and what a good family for Gungi to be given into. It seems impossible to get rid of her."

The meaning was clear. It was about Kamala that

* Pilgrimages.

they were talking, and she winced as she heard those words and thought of running away. But where could she go? Why was she born? In her agony she unconsciously went to her father-in-law. It was he who had brought about the marriage and she would speak to him. She rushed in through the quadrangle to the side room where her father-in-law usually stayed. Trembling with excitement she fell at his feet. "Oh why did you get me married to your son? Why did you not ask for money? Did you not know that I was a beggar? Now all this trouble has come on me. No one will love me. Let me go to father." The words were uttered in a tone of agony.

"Hush, child, why are you so agitated?" said the solemn man in a tone of surprise. He stooped to raise her, saying, "Don't cry so. Who told you that you were poor and penniless? *We* have to look to that. You go and do your work." She was so child-like in rushing to him and crying that he forgot that she was a grown-up girl and stroked her face and said that she must not get all kinds of nonsense into her head. He did not expect that of a *shastri's* daughter. She must work to please her mother-in-law.

"Oh! He does not know and cannot understand what I have to bear," thought Kamala. "Father will say the same." And she went inside to her own room and almost sobbed her heart out. The whole thing was clear now. She was born to give trouble to others. She was a poor man's daughter and they wanted to get rid of her. That was the reason why she was so despised. And now her husband would also despise her. She tried to remember if her father ever spoke of money. Did he possess any? And if she asked him would he give her any? But how was she to see her father? And what was that about her mother? Did no one know her? Everything looked so dismal. Her happiness seemed to depart with the evening light, and there was darkness in her soul. While she was thinking thus, some one happened to enter the room. The light of the window fell on the face and figure of a young man. He said: "Mother! mother!" Kamala turned and looked full at him. Was it her husband, who had been expected, that had returned? And the thought that he too had come to despise her sent a pang through her. In a voice that was full of pain and scarcely audible she said: "Mother is not here."

"And who are you in the dark corner? Get up."

Kamala rose shyly and said, "It is I." The light from the window fell full on her as she stood there, and revealed to him what seemed a vision of beauty. It was now two years since Ganesh left his girl-bride, and he was quite taken aback at the sight of a tall, slim, but handsome girl, with tears trembling on her long dark eyelashes and her white rounded cheeks. Her soft fair face seemed as if it were lit by a moonbeam. "Are you Kamala?" he exclaimed, and Kamala looked up with surprise and her gaze went through him, so child-like in its helpless innocence and confiding trust it seemed. He turned away as if he did not care, but he felt a yearning in his heart to say a kind word to the startled girl.

CHAPTER VI.

AFTER her husband's return there was no change for the better in Kamala's lot, only the daily routine of work became harder and she was kept more in the background. Kamala's duties commenced very early in the morning. She slept in her mother-in-law's room, a dark dingy room lighted by only one window at the top and full of little niches in the wall. In one of the niches were kept her simple toilet things, a *kunkun* box, a shell-comb, and a hand mirror. In another were placed wreaths of flowers of jessamine, or *shivanti*, and a betel-nut box and tray. Her clothes were hung on a rod which was fastened across the room; and two wooden boxes formed the only furniture. In the darkest corner were Kamala's own little bundle of clothes and her mattress rolled up by it. In the morning, long before day-break, there was a stir in the house, and the mother-in-law would wake the girl who slept near her. Thus aroused Kamala hurried out through the quadrangle to the back of the house, for it was her duty to get the water vessels ready and fill them with water for the morning ablutions. Then came the cow-dunging of the kitchen and front yard, and the working out of various flower designs on the cow-dunged floor with white shell powder, at which difficult feat every Hindu girl is an expert. Next came the buying of vegetables and other things from street vendors and the work in the kitchen, where she was expected to help in cooking. She was also required to prepare the baths, keep the ointments and other things ready, and if anything was missing a shower of abuse was hurled upon her. The food was served by Ramabai while Kamala stood looking on from behind a door. In the afternoons the older members of the family generally rested, whilst the girls attended to their toilet. They arranged their hair, wearing flowers in their tresses, and put *kunkun* on their foreheads. The hardest share of work fell on Kamala. She went through it willingly but she felt hurt when, after doing all that she could possibly do, her mother-in-law would come and say that poor Gungi's back was broken with work, and that Kamala required somebody to attend on her instead of taking her share in the general work and thus lightening the load of her sister-in-law. Then would come complaints from Ramabai that Kamala did not eat all the food that was served on her leaf. "She wants others to think that we starve her and that we are cruel to her. She puts on such an air of martyrdom before people that one feels inclined to scoop her eyes out." And the mother would pass Kamala with a scowl and a withering look and say: "Yes! the *Kydashin** will create more mischief still." Thus was kept up a long misunderstanding; and poor Kamala knew not how to defend herself or what to say. She was shocked at the lies told by her sisters-in-law and was dumb before them.

Somehow Kamala became resigned to her lot, and

* A term of abuse.

it was her crude religious convictions that enabled her to do so. She had sat at the *puranicbava's** feet and had imbibed the teachings taught by the heroic tales of Seeta, Rama, and the Pandavas. She had heard many a legend of demons and their power over human beings. The dreamy melodies of the Sanskrit *shlokas* had lulled her to sleep. The stories told her by old dames on moonlight nights, when, half asleep, she would with others press round the story tellers, were mainly in the manner of fables with a moral. The rivers and hills and trees were represented as personalities, and birds and beasts had tongues given to them. All these had taught her one lesson, the great lesson of humanity, love for others and the need of doing one's duty at any cost. However crude the stories and legends were they all shewed how good deeds were rewarded and bad deeds punished even in the next life, how humility had its reward, and love, chastity, honour, and respect for elders were looked upon as the distinguishing virtues of a noble life. This was the sum and substance of Kamala's moral code, and this gave her an impetus to be good. But there was another kind of teaching mingled with it all and that was that whether she was good or bad, whether she enjoyed pleasure or suffered pain, she ought not to grumble but accept it meekly, for it was her *fate*. This gave her very little consolation. It only made her feeble in purpose and in will. She lost even her simple interest in life; for life was a poor spiritless affair and whatever was written in the

* The interpreter of Puranas.

book of fate would come to pass do what she could to avert it. She wished to be exemplary like Savitri, Seeta, and other noble women; but even they had to submit to fate and did not get their due in this world. So Kamala reasoned while she bore meekly all the taunts and hard words of her sisters-in-law and wondered why she ever felt happy at all, as she did when she looked on the blue sky, the radiant sunset, or the swollen river,—why she felt such longing to be lost in a great wild wilderness, where she might dream in silence and enjoy to her heart's content the glory and the magnificence of earth and sky.

Kamala was not entirely absorbed in her own affairs. The lives of her girl friends were to her the objects of a great deal of interest and sympathy. She heard story after story of trials and troubles undergone by girls of her own age; and she often with her own eyes witnessed scenes which shocked her and gave her food for much painful reflection. In the opposite house, for instance, was Bhagirathi, suffering terrible persecution at the hands of her enraged husband, who thought that she had set at nought his orders and had openly defied him by leaving the house. She was a girl with some education and a great deal of spirit. Her husband, who was wealthy, but illiterate, did not care for her; and he slighted her in every way possible, ridiculing her learning and taking a delight in breaking her spirit, as he called it. She spent days and nights in great mental agony, and when he openly insulted her by bringing in a mistress she left the house, flinging aside the jewels which he had given her and even smashing the bangles on her wrists which were not to be removed so long as she lived. But, poor girl! she was not allowed to remain in her mother's house even for a day, lest her husband should cast her off for ever. So she was brought back disgraced, by her angry mother, who tried to act as peace maker. Kamala was returning from the well when Bhagirathi was brought back to her husband's house. Bhagirathi was writhing in anguish as she stood at the door with her mother, but nobody seemed to take any notice of them. The mother made a great noise and began abusing her. "There! See what you have brought yourself to, go in now," she said, pushing her.

"I won't go in, mother! You can kill me with your own hands, but I won't enter this living grave," she said, with quiet firmness. It was a painful sight to Kamala. A number of women gathered from the neighbouring houses, but very little sympathy was shown for Bhagirathi. One said mockingly: "What? You went away in such a temper and you have come back again." "Shame to you, girl," said another. "Don't you know that if a man be tied to you once, you cannot free yourself from him, even if he be an ass. The halter is round your neck, let it be wooden or golden, it is all the same." "What a fall," said a third triumphantly. "What jewels he gave you! Can't you at least be satisfied with them. Go inside and fall at his feet."

Bhagirathi did not answer, nor did she shew by any signs that she heard these remarks. She had at first a fixed scornful look, but afterwards she sat on the steps with her head bowed down. What pangs passed through her nobody knew. Kamala stood for some time looking at it all from afar. She was afraid of the people, but when she heard the cruel taunts she rushed to her friend with the water vessel in her hand. Just then the door opened and Bhagirathi's husband asked carelessly what the noise was about and then added: "Has the 'spit-fire' returned?" Bhagirathi rose quickly. Her breath came fast and quick, but she suppressed her sobs, and covering her head entered the house. Her face was full of determination, and she cast a withering look around her. When inside the house she turned to her mother who was apologizing for her conduct, and said: "Don't talk mother. Don't demean yourself any more. You have brought me back and nothing shall make me leave this house again alive. Go home."

The husband chuckled and said, "But who is going to take you in? She talks high. She has broken even the bangles which can only be removed after she is dead. Let her break the sacred knot round her neck as well."

Kamala went away heartsore and feeling a choking repugnance for the coarse and heartless man. She realized for the first time the extent to which a husband can tyrannize over his wife when he chooses to do so. She did not as yet understand, however, what pangs rend the heart of the wife who craves for love to find only hatred. She knew not how the better feelings of the soul are turned to bitterness and gall by looks, contempt, and insults undeserved.

There was, too, the fair looking Harni close by, who, though she belonged to a wealthy family and was blessed with a good husband, had a very ill-natured mother-in-law who tyrannized over the little girl in a shameful manner. Though brought up in luxury, Harni did not shrink from even the hardest work, but nothing that she could do pleased her mother-in-law. In fact the more pliable she was the more the mother-in-law hated her. Her husband tried all means to bring about peace and good will between them, but the more he interfered the more exasperated the old woman became, assigning all kinds of evil motives to his efforts at peace-making.

"He cares not for me. He loves her, and would like to see the chit of yesterday lord it over me. In one or two years she will drive me out of this house and she will have it all her own way. I shall be left in the street, I who brought up that boy and have made a man of him."

Harni heard such remarks daily and hourly. In the mornings when she was busy her mother-in-law would inquire in a harsh voice :—"What underhand work have you been doing to-day? What lies have you been telling about your mother-in-law? What secrets have you confided to your husband? He can't bear me, he who was so fond of me. You have thrown dust in his eyes, you have drugged him with draughts, so that his heart is against the mother that bore him." Then, irritated at Harni's calm demeanour, she would work herself into a frenzy and exclaim :—"Oh! the day will come when I shall see you dishonoured, trampled on, and it will soon come." And as a climax she would burst into tears and say: "The gods will have their revenge, on him also for his unnatural conduct," and cry loudly while the timid son would slink away from the house and go to his work. The poor girl, after weeping her eyes out and seeing her husband go out despondently to his work, would refuse to eat and thus provoke more grumblings from the old dame. When the grumblings became unbearable she would on pretext of bringing water, go to the well side with her brass pot. There she was sure to meet with some sympathy from her girl friends. They would gather round her to give her counsel and advice and cheer her up. But such comfort was only for a short time and then she would return home—a home made dark and dismal by the hatred and jealousy of a foolish ignorant woman.

But there were other girls, like Kashi and Rukhma, who were supremely happy in their homes. They went in and out among their friends spreading joy and happiness everywhere. Kashi had a dear mother who had a high sense of duty and was full of wisdom and goodness. She hated double-dealing and had little sympathy with weak people who were easily led by others. She pitied Kamala for having a mother-in-law who did not know how to manage her house and family. She knew how it would all turn out in the end for Kamala, how the first extravagant love and praise for the beautiful girl-bride would change into indifference and coldness, and then into hatred at the instigation of others. She loved Kamala from the beginning; for her truthful and innocent spirit quite won over the grand old dame, who regretted that because she had no son she could not take Kamala into her own family. She showed great wisdom and discretion in choosing a husband for Kashi, and affairs were so managed between the two families that there was no misunderstanding between them. Kashi was extremely happy in her husband's love, and her mother-in-law was as fond of her as her own mother. The two families lived near to each other, and the old dames regarded each other as sisters.

Rukhma, the *shastri's* daughter, was also intensely happy in her husband's home, though she was not so rich and highly connected as Kashi. Both these girls got their mothers to provide amusements for their less fortunate friends and came and took them away on the plea of feasts, festivals, and ceremonies to their own houses, thus bringing sunshine and happiness to girls whose lives were dark and dismal compared with their own.

The relations between a husband and a wife in an orthodox Hindu home are, as a general rule, much constrained. The two have not the same liberty of speech and action that are accorded to them usually in European countries. The joint family system is the chief cause of this anomalous state of things. The Hindu wife, unless she lives with her husband in a house of her own, scarcely exchanges a word with him before other members of the family. They behave as if they were strangers to each other, the woman covering her head at her husband's approach, or leaving the room when he happens to come in, or standing aside, and when talked to, either not taking any notice of what is said, or, with head turned aside, answering in the most distant manner possible. The mother-in-law's jealousy prohibits the young people from having anything like liberty of speech or action in her presence. Kamala had no desire to speak to her husband nor did she court any notice from him. At the marriage ceremony all eyes had been on them, and if they were at any time caught looking at each other the fact was made the subject of ridicule. After that Kamala had not seen her husband for a long time, and now she dared not lift her eyes in his presence. This was due not merely to false shyness but to the feeling that she was a creature to be despised and ill-treated. Hence it was that she avoided her husband as much as possible. She, however, had opportunities of watching him. He was very fond of his mother and often sat by her, petted by her. When anything took her to the room where he was he would look at her frankly as if she was his property, and this brought a flush of shame to her face, but she drove away any feeling of regard for him by saying to herself:—"He will not long take an interest in me. He will despise me when he finds out that I am low and poor and that I have not a soul in the world to care for me." But her husband's interest in her deepened the more she recoiled into herself. He wondered why when girls of her age craved for flowers and jewels and courted admiration she was so perfectly indifferent. His mother had often hinted that as a *sanyasi's* daughter she had lost all the instincts of civilized life and behaved differently from other girls. Was this all true ? Was she really without feeling ? The thought of Kamala being unlike other girls disheartened him, but as he observed her more closely he found that the immobility of countenance and indifference of look were not natural but were due to a long course of wrong suffered by her at the hands of his sisters. His mother, he knew, was easily led by her daughters. Already she had begun to make remarks to him about Kamala, whom she accused of being ungrateful and obstinate and not having any regard for his sisters, who, she made out, were most kind to Kamala. "They are not like other sisters-in-law," she would say. "They teach her work which will be most useful to her hereafter, but she has no love for them, and behaves still as a stranger."

CHAPTER VII.

GANESH found out that his sisters gave Kamala all the drudgery to do. This was done, it was said, to make her hardy. Before strangers, however, it was all "Poor Girl! No mother;" and it was made out that the daughters were managing the house all by themselves. He also accidentally discovered one evening why the girl looked so feelingless and indifferent. Kamala was not aware of the interest she was exciting in her husband and it was only by chance that she found this out. It was a hot dusky day and she knew not why she felt ill and feverish. All the girls of the neighbouring houses had met for play in an open space, but she had no mind to join them. She had found a cool nook for herself behind a small ruined temple that stood between her house and the river, and there she sat feeling very miserable. She did not know that she had a burning fever and was there a long time sitting with her throbbing head in her lap when somebody seemed to approach her. She was too tired to lift up her head, and it was only when she was touched that she started with surprise, for the touch on her head was soft and caressing and the words that fell were sympathetic.

"What, not well? What are you doing here?" Kamala's eyes opened with astonishment and dread as she looked on the face she had avoided, for it was her husband who was standing by her side. "Don't be mad, I am not going to eat you up. Come near, let me feel you. You are hot and feverish."

At this she opened her eyes wider with astonishment and when he approached her she shrank and drew her head away with great agitation saying :—"You are not to touch me, you know, and you are not to talk to me," and she tried to hide her face and get away.

"Who told you all this?" he asked with a smile, detaining her. "Don't be foolish. Now go in and take care of yourself. Tell mother that you have fever, and take medicine. I knew you were foolish and that is why I came to search for you."

"You search for me?" she asked.

"Yes! I missed you the whole day and wanted to see you," he said, stooping down to look into her face. She looked more surprised than ever, but after a little while she gazed into his face, and with trembling lips and glistening eyes said :—"Will you not also despise me like the others and wish me away?"

"No! why should I? What thoughts are in your head?"

"Because I am poor and penniless," the girl said, "and I have nobody to go to." She broke down as she uttered these words and began to cry. The interest and sympathy shown by her husband had touched the springs of her heart and she unconsciously unburdened her mind to him. Tears came fast but she was not afraid to show them. Kind words and looks had done their work, and she forgot everything and talked to him as to a friend.

"Father does not come to see me," she said.

"I will bring the *sanyasi* to you, and you must not give way like this. Nobody despises you. What do you know of money? I have to get that for you." He wiped her eyes with her *saree,* at which she felt shy again and went in with her head down and her heart full of new emotions while he struck out to the river bank for a stroll. Her head was throbbing with pain, and as she went in she laid herself down in her own room. There was joy in her heart. She had found a friend at last when she least expected one. Her head ached more and the fever rose, but she cared not; she scarcely felt ill, for somebody there was who cared for her.

That night she saw lights dancing round her and the room full of people, and felt the touch of many hands, but was not able to distinguish whose they were. After that she knew nothing till days afterwards, when she opened her eyes and felt the bracing mountain winds around her. Some one was feeling her pulse. Two eyes were earnestly fixed on her and the power of those eyes transfixed her so that she could not turn away. The man had one hand on her pulse and the other on her forehead, and waves of new power seemed to pass from him to her. Her morbid excitement left her. She felt soothed and strengthened and closed her eyes. "She is better," said the young man, relinquishing his hold. "I have had a great struggle, let her sleep." The voice was so soft and the firm touch on the forehead so soothing, that she slept for hours together, and when she got up she realized, for the first time, that she was in a strange place—a cool temple cloister with bells ringing, interrupted at intervals by the boom of gongs and the shrill sound of conch shells. Her mother-in-law, her husband, and Kashi all were near. The priest came, chanted *mantras* and burnt incense, and waving *margosa* leaves over her said that the bewitching influence was gone, mysteriously adding: "Seven shares had been made of her body but the *grahadevas* (house deities) and our great goddess refused to take shares and so she has been spared." He asked them to have the sick girl bathed in the sacred tank in front and to present further offerings to the goddess. Kamala, however, gathered from the conversation of those present that it was not the *mantras* of the priest but the skill of the strange young man who had such influence over her that wrought the cure. All day long she heard nothing but praise of him and his wonderful medicines.

"We thought that you were not going to live," said Kashi, putting her hand round Kamala. "The fever did not leave you for days together They tried every means and failed, and were at last told by a woman, who, in a trance, invoked the aid of the spirit of a departed relative, that you were bewitched and that Kunniah, the virgin spirit, had got hold of you, and they brought you here to be exorcised. But after coming here you became cold and lifeless, and messages came to me, those terrible messages—you know what they mean, my Kamala! I hastened here with father who brought the young man with him, for he knew his skill, and see what it has done for you."

Next day the young man came again. Kamala felt awed in his presence and a strange power seemed to hold her again in his grasp. She felt that she would do anything that this man ordered, and she trembled at the thought. It was when he was about to go that she recognised to her surprise that he was the stranger she had met near the mountain home gathering herbs and whom she had taken to her father. But she kept this knowledge to herself, afraid to tell others. After a time her strength returned and she was taken back to her home. Her husband was unremitting in his care and attention. This roused much opposition but he did not mind. Feeble and weak she accepted his attentions with great gratitude. She knew that her mother-in-law and sisters-in-law were displeased. They were angry because her husband in defiance of all rules had taken upon himself the task of nursing her. They resented his coming into the sick room to enquire about her; but Kamala was too weak to do any thing to pacify them.

Among the Hindus it is customary to pay a visit once a year to various sacred places which they look upon as the favourite abodes of their numerous deities. Women and children meet together, prepare cakes and sweetmeats to last them for days, and then set out in carts, sometimes going long distances before reaching their destination. Among places of pilgrimage Dudhasthal is justly famed, and people go to it from far and near. It is itself a spot of great beauty and there are many similar spots in its neighbourhood. Here Ganga Godavari converges and leaps down from a huge rock into a rocky cavern below, forming a very beautiful waterfall. The water, falling on a rocky slab in the cavern, breaks into spray, which rises, and appears in the distance like a soft white fleecy cloud. It is for this reason that the place has received its name, for Dudhasthal means 'milky spot.'

To Dudhasthal a large party went from Sivagunga every year. The time for the pilgrimage was drawing nigh as Kamala was recovering from her illness, and when the party set out she went too. Kashi and several more of her girl friends were with her and she was intensely happy. She joined now one group and now another and enjoyed herself to her heart's content. The freedom and innocent pleasure such journeys afford are in striking contrast to the dull, artificial surroundings of Hindu homes. Kamala cared not what her sisters-in-law thought of her. They were there, but they had no power over her. Her instinctive love of nature was thoroughly satisfied, for many and varied were the rural scenes she witnessed.

The dewy woodlands through which the pilgrims pass in the mornings echo to the sound of the woodman's axe, and the splash of water being drawn by bullocks is heard in the distance. Sounds come, too, from Arcadian spots, where the purple clusters of the vine are seen drooping through light green leaves, and the flowers of the orange and the lemon waft their sweetness on the air. Nearer the wells are seen greens and vegetables growing in long luxuriant beds, and human voices begin to be distinctly heard. Perhaps a damsel is passing by with a load of fruit or vegetables, and the youthful peasant who is driving the bullocks sings out to her in mocking rhymes. He asks her to turn round and taste of his water :—"Drink, and your thirst will be quenched, your face gather new beauty, and grace; for such is the liquid I draw out for you." Then the "Hakya! Hakya!" to the bullocks, as he spurs them on to walk faster is heard echoing and re-echoing from the hills around. The retort of the damsel to the daring peasant is lost in the wind as she hurries through the grove: "My song is locked in a box, thou long-tongued man, but take care that thou for lack of words, hast not to borrow from it, for those who do so fare badly indeed......" The peasant heeds not the girl but goes on with his song. As the pilgrims approach the fields, the scent of flowers, or of the new mown hay, or of the upturned earth overcomes them. They hear a merry challenge as they pass by, for men and women vie with each other, amid much hilarity, in gathering the bundles of hay and binding them together in heaps. Further on they hear the tramp of feet keeping time to rhymed songs sung with great gusto by a chorus of male voices. These are the labourers returning with their loads to their homes. Listen to their songs. "Lightly, lightly, step up boys," come from one group. "Hoi! Hoi!" is the answer from another. "Now o'er mounds, now o'er dales." "Hoi! Hoi!" "Now to our homes, where fried cakes are cheap, where the silly women folks wait our coming." "Hoi! Hoi!" And then as a pretty woman happens to pass by the song and the tune change suddenly:—

"Was it a black *saree* that did the work?" "Nay! Nay!" "Or the fawn-like eyes or steps like the hind's?" "Yes! Yes!" come the answer, and there is a loud laugh. The poor woman just approaching turns aside with her head down, while the song becomes more mischievous. "Modest face and modest eyes!" "Hoi! Hoi!" "That is what I love!" "Yes! Yes!" "Stop your foolery, or your ears will tingle," says the woman, but only a loud "Hoi! Hoi!" is heard from over the hills where the men have already gone. The long procession mingling with the clouds has a weird effect on the passers by. The labourers' village is far below, and their wives and children eagerly waiting for them excuse their passing mirth. It is their hard toil, and the free air that they breathe which breed such innocent cheerfulness in their hearts.

Now the pilgrims pass by a dreamy *tapa* tank over which the lotus bows its modest head. Lazy cattle are sleeping on its banks, and the hum of bees is heard on all sides. In the grove near by is a deity of greater or less sanctity according to the number of huge stone-carved figures in front. A solemn Buddha is sleeping not far away, either in a grove or on a mound overlooking the scene. The travellers as they proceed come across a few ill-built huts surrounding a crudely built temple from which are seen peeping the ashen figures of *bhairagis*. After making their obeisance to the deity they pass on, and soon find themselves standing in front of a rocky cave, overgrown with creepers. They hear the continual drip drip of the water that wells out from the sides of the cave. The cool refreshing air greets them as they peep in, one after the other, and the pellucid waters received in the clear basin below quench their thirst. This is Seeta's bath, and the rude slab of rock cut in the shape of a cot with moss-grown stones underneath and ferns springing up on all sides is the cradle of her babe. It is a hilly place, and monkeys chatter in the gigantic trees round about and throw the stones of *jambul* and other fruits in merry mischief on the passers by. Further on the travellers hear the sound of the *tom-tom*. A god has visited the place and all the villagers close by are hastening thither. A tree cut by a reckless wood-man's axe has shown signs of the god's presence, for, behold, through the wound made by the axe the blood gushes out. Already a goat has been killed to appease the wrath of the god, flags are being raised on all sides, and soon a primitive shrine of stones will be erected. Kamala sees all, gathers the forest flowers with her friends, and at every shrine and temple visited, she offers her gifts and prays her prayer:—"O God! befriend me, help and protect my father, and grant me happiness." Her heart is moved to greater awe the more hideous the deity she is worshipping.

In the day-time the pilgrims stopped their carts in a tope or grove under huge spreading trees or by the side of some tank or stream. Fires were lit and every one lent a helping hand in cooking the simple meal. All would join in bringing water and collecting fuel, and many a hilarious talk would be carried on and many a joke cracked at the expense of the younger members. The men were very few compared with the women, as is the case in all such pilgrim bands. But among the men was Kamala's husband. Kashi, Bhagirathi, and some other girls were much older than Kamala, so she had to bear the brunt of the teasing, for she had to do many a little task for her husband before her girl friends. There was an innocent, happy familiarity between them all. When drawing water from any deep well, the men gladly came forward to help the damsels, not minding to which group or separate family they belonged. In the evenings, before nightfall, the pilgrims would stop at some inn, and there they would rest for the night. The familiar lowing of cattle and the sight of houses brought a peculiar sense of restful peace to Kamala. She would sit by Kashi and hear her talk, dreamily gazing at the stars and listening to the howling of the winds in the ill-protected rest-house. Her husband always sought her out in the evenings and would sit by her sometimes and describe to her and to Kashi and her mother the various places of interest they had visited during the day.

CHAPTER VIII.

THE pilgrim band reached Dudhasthal, the furthest point of their journey, after spending about eight days in visiting various places by the way. Kamala was much impressed with the sight that met her eyes and with the loud roar of the rushing waters that fell upon her ears. The breeze came in gusts, making a hoarse melody. The voice of the forest was loud, and the hills echoed back the rush of the waters. Quaint little dwellings built of rounded stone and slabs were visible all round. At a distance from the waterfall the river broadened and just washed the feet of a huge *Nundi* (the sacred bull) carved in stone that stood aloof, frowning on all. The temple was in a dark grove all by itself a little away from the river. Kamala listened to the talk of the women about her. Some were throwing fried rice into the river, and some were breaking cocoanuts, while the elderly ones made quite a hue and cry as they saw the river leaping into the cavern below. "Hari! Hari! Shiva! Shiva!" exclaimed the pious ones, "our sacred Ganga is being swallowed by the earth. There are enemies all around. Even Mother Earth is jealous of her good deeds and tries to thwart her in her good course." Kamala was in the thick of the crowd standing on the steps very near to the dizzy rush of waters. The place had awakened sensations which she felt she had experienced before. She seemed to think that she was looking at an old familiar scene. The feeling was most powerful as she stood on the brink of the rushing river. There was a rock opposite to her, and she recognised it distinctly. She had heard the rush of the waters before. Surely she had seen it all. But what had happened there? Why that dreamy pain in her head? It was a throb of anguish. She seemed to have fallen into a trance, for who was it she saw near her leading her by the hand? It was the form of a noble lovely woman who wore a diamond bracelet. The waters hissed and roared round her, and in a moment she felt her foot slip and herself carried forward. Then she seemed to see the woman plunge after her with a cry. The dreadful pool, ah! how dark it looked! A dart of pain passed through her. She was grasped and pulled out by the woman, but when was it and where? Had she really once gone through it all before? What was it that brought it all so vividly to her recollection? While thus absorbed, a voice fell on her ears and she started. It was her father's voice which had strangely mingled with the vivid picture her mind had formed. It was like a strain of long forgotten music casting a spell on her and round her, and now it struck her ears distinctly as she seemed to awake as it were from her dream. She turned round with a great effort and just then she saw her father's form disappear in the crowd. She cried:—"Father! Father!" and ran through the crowd. But what became of her father? For at the farthest end of the surging crowd she found herself alone on the steps of a temple in a dark grove. The sound of gongs and shells was deafening. Fear overcame her at the strange scene, and the crowd of faces round her looking at her curiously. "Oh! what will my husband say and my mother-in-law if they see me here alone?" she thought. The ashen figures of the *bhairagis* and the large staring eyes of the hideous looking priests made her feel uncomfortable. She was terror-struck, aud the dreadful thought of spells cast over damsels came over her and she would have screamed, but she felt all her power gone and she sank on the ground. "Rise," said a voice calm, composed, and authoritative, and she obeyed with a shudder. "Come to your people, this is no place for you. Your father is gone." At this she looked up, and whom should she see but the young physician? A sudden calm came over her. She tried to say something.

"Hush! don't talk! This is not the place to talk," and so saying he grasped her hand firmly and led her through the crowd to a group far from the others. It was Kashi's group, and Kamala breathed freely as she saw Kashi approaching her.

"Narayen, the *sanyasi*, told me to ask you to take Kamala to her people. He is there in the temple and saw you from a distance, but has other duties just now." Having said this the man left. This speech took Kamala's breath away, and she could not say anything to Kashi, who had looked at her inquiringly, and when Kamala began to cry Kashi thought that it was due to the parting with her father and comforted her, and then they all went to join Kamala's own people, who were still on the raised bank. This little incident disturbed Kamala considerably. What was it in her that gave rise to such visions? Had she really witnessed the scene once before, and why had her father disappeared? She had heard of visions and trances, but she feared to tell this to anyone. Was it a message from the goddess, the noble river deity? Oh! what would Kashi say if she told her all, and who was this man who said he was commissioned by her father? Kamala felt grateful to him and grew more and more troubled, but kept it all to herself.

Ganesh saw much of Kamala during this journey, for there was not then the same fettered relation between him and his wife as there was in the house. Many were the stolen conversations he had with her, and he daily became more and more enamoured of her. There was a certain grace and refinement about her which together with her unique beauty marked her out as distinct from other girls of her age. He found her, moreover, eager to get information about everything, and wonderfully quick of comprehension, and with the English ideas he had imbibed regarding women's love and education he thought of striking ont a new line and developing Kamala's mind and so training her to be a real companion to him.

With this object in view he took the training of his wife into his hands immediately after they returned from the *yatra*. The obstacles in the way were great. His mother and sisters disapproved of his conduct and accused him of forgetting his manhood; for, said they, what man with any self-respect would make much of his wife, give her learning, and raise her up to his own level? The wife, as the saying went, was 'the cat under the plate,' the slave of the family and of her lord. They considered that he was disgracing himself in acting thus. Ganesh for a time assumed a bold attitude and tried to follow his own way. But his mother put on a grief-stricken air and showed a wounded pained face as if some great personal wrong had been done to her. She would sometimes cry before her son and upbraid him in words like these:—"What is it that has come over you. Why do you make an idol of the girl? You have stopped her from working and have put books into her hands as if she were going to earn her bread. Why was I born into this world to see such things. How hurt your sisters are! She has no feeling for us, no love. It is she that has put you up to all this. We knew that she was fond of reading."

"Oh, mother! Why do you say such hard things? Do you think an hour or so devoted in the mornings to reading will make her all that you describe. I only want her to be a little more of a companion to me. She won't lord it over you. In fact learning will teach her humility, and she can work after her lessons are over. When the food is cooked for all, could you not give her a little? Why need you say that you have all to work for her?"

But she was not to be pacified, and she would pull a face and sit disconsolate in a corner. It went to Ganesh's heart to see his mother so sad, and he would try his best to soothe and coax her. When dinner was served, his mother, who used before to sit in front of him and watch him eat, would now leave him and go into another room. It was a hard time for Ganesh, for his father, too, changed in his behaviour to him. The old man was in the habit of holding long conversations with his son about college life, and would take a delight in ridiculing the new learning or would sit hours together going into raptures over some piece of Vedantic literature. But now he sat in sullen silence, and whenever anything was said by Ganesh he would merely give an unwilling grunt. Ganesh was avoided, too, by his sisters, who would stand aside talking to their mother in whispers. The only person who appeared to behave naturally was Ramabai's husband, for he was somehow assiduous in his attentions to Ganesh. Kamala of course was the greatest sufferer. She noticed the averted faces and heard covert sneers and abuses, and her heart sank within her, but she did not for a long time know what offence she had committed. When she, as usual, went to assist in the domestic work, no one took any notice of her, and even the most insignificant work was rudely taken from her. One day when she went to the kitchen to take her food, for it was here that the female members generally took their meals, she found none for herself. She stood and waited for some time, but nobody, not even the servant woman, took any notice of her. She was very hungry, but she did not open her mouth. In the evening when she went to the well, Rukhma asked her why she looked so cast down. Happy Rukhma did so in her usual jovial, chiding manner and tears came to Kamala's eyes when she felt she had to tell her all. She simply said that she had no food and was very hungry. Rukhma at once put down her vessel and ran to her house and brought some cakes which she had herself prepared, and coaxed Kamala to eat. Kamala felt as if she would choke, but with difficulty she swallowed a little. "Why did you not receive food?" Rukhma asked. Kamala said that she did not know. There was something wrong, she said, and she was afraid to ask anybody, and she also added that she had not been given any work of late and that all in the house had avoided her. It seemed a mystery to both. After a few moments' silence, Rukhma said, "What will you do if this goes on?" Kamala again broke down and cried, and her companion wiped away her tears. Rukhma asked her not to tell anybody, but to come to the well side after dinner and share some cakes with her every day.

What would Kamala's father have said if he had seen his darling daughter then, he who had done his best to keep her free from every kind of work? She had never felt any want as long as she lived with him and her life with him had been one long dream of happiness. But as it was with Kamala, so it usually is in Hindu families. Once given over, the daughter so lovingly brought up, is no more the concern of her parents. It is improper for them to interfere in any way with her new life, for what is written in the book of fate comes to pass.

By chance Kamala learned that her food was served

in the men's quarter. The servant woman it was that gave her this information, for she could not bear to see Kamala's starved face. She, too, was indignant with Kamala, and told her that it was her own conduct that brought all this on her. Kamala did not know what to make of it all, and questioned her husband afterwards about it. He told her that all this came of his having begun to teach her. Kamala then asked to be excused. "You don't know what I have to bear," she said, "have pity on me." But he told her not to mind anything, and that he was determined to go on with the lessons. He was for a time very kind and loving and taught her regularly in the mornings, and those were happy times for Kamala, in spite of all opposition. But there came a change in her husband's behaviour, and he gradually left off coming to teach her. Kamala had nothing to do in the mornings; but she was afraid to leave her room and go to work again as usual, for many were the bitter shafts directed against her in the women's quarter. Day after day she waited at the appointed hour for her husband to come and teach her, but he did not come. She did not know how to account for this change in him and she felt indignant at his conduct. She had not cared for the other people and had learnt to put up with their treatment of her, but now when she found that the only person whom she regarded as her friend was beginning to be indifferent, the disappointment was indeed keen. Her pride was touched, for this was a downfall for her. She had felt a certain reposeful confidence in her husband which now was replaced by a weak distrust. Many a taunt and covert sneer now flew past her as she left her room, and smiles and words distinctly said: "Ah! what a fall. What was the use of so much ado and what has come of all your intrigue!" She felt sorely hurt. In vain she tried to find excuses for her husband's conduct. "He cannot help it," she thought, "it is probably his mother's and sister's doing." But such thoughts gave her no comfort. In the meantime, however, there was a change in the behaviour of the other members of the family. They did not give vent to their hatred of Kamala in any open manner, and they seemed to make much of her husband and take great pleasure in his company, and she felt glad for him, though for herself she knew there would never be any pardon. This change was brought about by Ramabai's husband. He was the family counsellor. When the female members found that what he had predicted with regard to Ganesh's relation to Kamala and to the family had come to pass, they went to her father-in-law and upbraided him for bringing such a girl into the family. "He is madly in love with her," said the mother, "he does not care for you or for anybody else, and outrages our feelings by showing such preference for her. He won't let her work and wants us to be her slaves." Such were the complaints they made.

The old man heard all, reflected, and was troubled, but Ramabai's husband came to his rescue. "I knew what it would all come to. These are the new-fangled ideas. I have been observing and have warned you more than once. But why, then, do you go on like this?

The more you oppose him the more he will be set on educating his wife, as he calls it. He will think he is fighting for his rights and your conduct will only alienate him from us. What does he care ? He will take her away if he finds that you are all against her. So now give him full liberty to do as he likes. Don't oppose him in any way, but on the other hand humour him in every way and hide your resentment to the girl. There are a thousand and one ways of diverting a young man's attention from his wife. I can see he is fond of pleasure and society. Try, therefore, to take him to temples and feasts, and so displace the new madness that is in him. When he finds no real opposition, he will put off the education of his wife, as he calls it."

They all assented, and the old man only said with a pained voice that he did not believe that his son would behave so foolishly, and that the girl he thought so much of would have encouraged him to publicly disobey his mother and attempt to alienate him from his own people. After this conversation Ganesh's mother beamed kindly on him and did not allude in any way to what she considered his disobedient conduct. His conscience smote him for having displeased so good a mother. "Her love is so great that she tolerates even this unpardonable conduct," he thought to himself, and then, moreover, as he was going away shortly to Rampur, he thought he could do the teaching there. So he gave up coming to instruct Kamala. He did not even seek her company as formerly, and he entered joyfully into the spirit of the diversions that were so cleverly prepared for him by his scheming relatives.

CHAPTER IX.

THERE were heights and depths in Kamala's nature, which no one knew and of which she herself was unconscious. The 'open sesame' had not been uttered. The torrents confined by artificial barriers lay still and dark. The strength of the floods no one had tested, and their sweeping vehemence had not begun to shew itself. Hitherto she was the placid, dreamy, bewildered, passive Kamala, the toy and prey of circumstances, submitting quietly to every tyranny, bearing calmly every new load of suffering as if everything was the outcome of fate. She was herself astonished at the way she was drifting along, doing the things that she was bidden to do, like the dumb mule, questioning no one, nor inquiring into the why or the wherefore of anything.

Somehow the conduct of her people did not trouble her much at this time. Her eyes had been opened gradually, and once disgusted with their meanness and their underhand dealings, she expected nothing good from them, and regarded their treatment of her as nothing extraordinary. But it was different with Ganesh; for though her feelings towards him had not as yet ripened into love, she had begun to regard him already as a friend and comrade. She felt that he was superior to his people. His conduct had justified her belief and trust in him. To have such a person as her husband, was it not a rare happiness?

So she thought, and tried to satisfy her longing throbbing heart. But why did her heart beat so wildly now and then? What did it long for? This friendship had awakened springs of new affection and had given birth to thoughts which startled her not a little, and which seemed to belong to a new world altogether—a world where it would be possible to live an ideal life, where perfect unity of sentiment would exist, and where each would understand the other's feelings and each would live for the other. Her feelings were vague and indistinct, but they were at times very strong. The persecution to which Ganesh and she had been subjected for some time had tightened the bonds between them. She sympathised and felt for him, even though he knew it not, and she wondered whether he too felt the same sympathy for her. Then she began to experience strange longings for something more than friendship. What did it mean? She questioned herself. But in vain she waited, longed, and pined. One look from him at that time, one sympathetic word, one loving touch would have opened the flood gates of her soul. As it was Ganesh kept away. Kamala, frightened at her thoughts, wondered at his coldness towards her, but thought it her duty to care for him, and to watch over him as a mother would watch over her son. Many little things were happening to disturb her, and her fears were often aroused. Was Ganesh coming to any trouble? She had already acquired an experience of the world that showed her where the quicksands of life lay, which those who wish to get on in this world must avoid.

Sai had come, and this was one of the chief sources of Kamala's troubles.

Sai Zadhovini, who was more generally known as Sai, whom Ganesh met casually at Rampur, at the dramatic performance, paid a visit to Sivagunga, where she had some property. On the evening of her arrival she was sitting in the verandah of her garden house at Sivagunga with some of her female attendants, when the sound of footsteps was heard.

"Halloa! who is there?" she asked loudly.

"Ram! Ram! Bai Sahib!" said a tall stalwart Bheel, approaching with a deep salaam.

"What is the news, Bheemiah?"

"All is going on well with your favour and God's mercy."

"So! So! How did the affair of the theft end?"

"Ha! Ha! The poor man did not know how to get out of the difficulty. He cursed his stars and said 'twas all Sai. I was, with your permission, under the trees and heard all the swearing and cursing. The vessels and valuables were found under his own grass *gunjee*. What a sell for him who wished to show off his detective powers by trying to trap the Bheels on the hills!"

"Serves him right," said Sai. "He did not take my advice. "On whose shoulders does he rest the blame of the theft now?"

"He has not done anything. He only wishes to see you and consult you. The whole village is astir. People walk the streets anxiously and no one thinks his property safe."

"All would have come right if he had left the matter to me and waited as I told him to do. What a humiliation this must be for him after all the ado he made in tracking the Bheels, when he finds the whole property secreted under his very nose? You are indeed valuable servants and you shall be rewarded. But what about Shunker Rau?" added Sai, turning the conversation to another subject. "Did he find his way back through the woods? Did I not send him the right way? Does the simpleton still believe that his mistress ran away from him? Be very close about this matter and I shall reward you handsomely! Not a word, mind you. The swell young man, the stranger, why does he still linger in these parts? You said he had some valuable jewels and passed through your hills."

"We know nothing of his whereabouts as yet, Bai Sahib. He now and then puts on the mendicant's garb to deceive us. But we shall yet find out and let you know. One of us met him leaving the hills dressed quite differently and on horseback, and all that means money and servants." Here another stalwart Bheel put in: "He will have to be careful of Dhondia, though, for I watch the pass on that side."

"All right, Bheemia, Dhondia," said Sai. "You may go now. I stay here for a fortnight. I shall be back at Rampur on the new moon day and then cross the stream to Agnai by Friday. Meet me at Sadashiva Dholl on the second day after the new moon. Give this to Aprathi the old woman, and tell her to have my room ready. Also tell Gondan that I may need my pony at the Dholl, Ram! Ram! *Kabar Dhar!*"

The above conversation gives a clue to the character of the woman. She was intimately connected with most of the mysterious things, such as robberies and quarrels, that happened in and about the district. She had attendants and trusty servants who kept her informed of all important events that took place in different localities. To outsiders she seemed a woman of great ability and power, and she was often entrusted with work, belonging to others, as for example, the detection of robbery and the settling of disputes. She always employed strangers who came with her own agents to see her, professedly on various errands. She would request them to buy something or other, now an old lace *saree*, or a jewel of a certain kind, addressing them as her own friends, and giving them the necessary instructions as to how to proceed. These tasks she imposed on them in such a free and jovial manner that even the rude rustics felt at ease in her presence. Government officials, too, consulted her now and then, and her advice and suggestions were eagerly carried out. Considering that such was her influence wherever she went, it was not surprising that she should have been acquainted with Ramabai's husband, who was himself a shrewd man of business. He was one of the first to be sent for by Sai when she came to Sivagunga. Ganesh was anxious to see her, and yet feared to come under her influence. So he kept at first in the background, but being persuaded by Ramabai's husband, he went with him to her house. There was quite a large number of people waiting to see her, and Ganesh mingled with them and peeped inside to see for himself what Sai was doing.

"Oh! who is this? This is a new face," she said eagerly. Ganesh would have withdrawn, but Ramabai's husband put his hand on his shoulder, and said, "This is my brother-in-law who has come home to spend some time with us; he has taken an extension of leave and stays here for Gungi's marriage."

"Oh, indeed," said Sai, lifting her eyebrows and eyeing him pleasantly with a smile on her face. "That was your lovely wife whom I saw at Dudhasthal? Don't be shy. Uncommon girl, but not of this side. Mind I know more about her than you do; and that was the quarrel sometime ago between you and your people? How is her education going on? Oh, there is no hiding," she said, as Ganesh looked startled. "We know all about it, could anything be a secret to Sai? I should like to see her again, but take care, she is a *sanyasi's* daughter." Saying this she waved an adieu with her hand as they were departing.

Poor Ganesh! His breath was almost taken away by her talk. He felt excited at the notice she had taken of him; and was surprised that *she* should want to see Kamala. How ignorant, innocent, and strange Kamala would look beside her? And what would Kamala think of this woman? He shuddered at the thought. Just then Ramabai's husband, as if reading his thoughts broke in: "Do you see now the difference between being educated and uneducated? Whom would you like to have as a wife? A simple, innocent modest girl afraid to open her mouth, or a bold, clever woman wielding such a dreadful power over others as this woman wields? Yet it is education that has made her what she is. She was dissatisfied with her home and her stupid loutish husband, and rumour has it that she poisoned him. Anyhow nobody knows what became of him. She has learnt to her heart's content and now she excels any man in accounts, and as for reading character no philosopher even could equal her. She is independent as a queen and cares not for common folks such as you and me, for she has princes for her friends. Now, do you see what it all means? Do you perceive that the great rise and the great fall are combined in her. I suppose you don't care. Your new learning trains women to be free, but what does it do for their morals? You would not mind, perhaps, seeing your lovely Kamala like this? You have only to stir her up and the sleeping waters of her soul will soon burst over all. And what will you be, Ganesh? Do you mean to say she will care for you? You will be only one of her many admirers who will make *poojah* to her. Did you not hear the note of alarm in her talk when she said: 'Take care of a *sanyasi's* daughter?' "

"Pooh! what care I for her alarms? Don't talk to me in that way? What do you know of Kamala? I admit that education and freedom do not do for all women, and there may be some sense in your talk, but all women are not Sais. Are you not aware of the innate sense of nobility that dwells in human souls, making them abhor everything that is mean, despicable, and low? Women love and honour those above them when their minds open to grasp the great and noble qualities they see in others. They cherish the loving hand that raises them up, and though elevated even to a throne they will do their best so to walk as never to grieve the tender heart that loves them and raises them. I am sure Sai never knew love."

"Well done! You have spoken boldly, yea, nobly, but what woman, her heart full of jealousy, her mind constantly bent on admiration, will ever rise so, I should like to know? Try the experiment and let us see whether you will succeed? Ninety-nine out of a hundred have others besides their husbands to love. But let us go in, for we have now reached home."

One of the objects of Sai's visit to Sivagunga was to be present at the great car festival that was about to be held in that city. The festival was an important one and people came from far and near. The car was decorated and was drawn out into the quadrangle of the temple of Bhagvani, which stood a little away from the city. It was a monstrous, barbaric chariot, blazing with tinsel and gold, and drawn by huge wooden horses about twice the size of ordinary animals. These were draped in fantastic colours and had mimic wooden figures of men and demons seated on their backs. Cart loads of offerings of all kinds had been prepared to propitiate the god, in order to facilitate the movement of the car through the city.

The scene at early dawn was one of the intensest excitement. Before cockcrow people with their offerings all ready were gathered in the enclosures and the groves around the temple, eager to catch the first glimpse of the moving car. At first there was a great stillness, but soon the cocks began to crow and there was life and animation in the crowd. The mothers in vain tried to hush the voices of their children by singing to them and pointing to the huge car which now towered in front dark and high, the living embodiment, as it were, of the prayers of the multitude. The light of dawn was met by a burst of music from the priests who stood ready in front of the car with soft sounding *veenas** and *tals** in their hands. The gentle soothing melody rose and fell, and was hailed as the benediction of the priests by the expectant multitude. Its long drawn notes were very unlike the usual noisy clanging of cymbals and the beating of *tom-toms*.

The sun rose, and then came the excitement of the moment, the offering of gifts. Fruits of all kinds, vegetables, flowers, fishes, goats, everything in fact that the people had brought, were offered, and nothing was despised. While the offerings were being presented there was a great uproar, followed by the jarring sounds of gongs and cymbals and the harsh beating of *tom-toms*. The people yelled frantically, caught hold of the huge ropes attached to the car, and pulled with all their might. But in spite of all the pulling, the car refused to move. Then the god was invoked. A woman rose and danced in front of the

* Hindu musical instruments.

car, exclaiming, "Govinda! Govinda!" "The God has come on her," said the people around. Then she spoke in a high shrill voice:—"Behold, I refuse to move, my heart is not satisfied. The field of gold I have, the waters of the universe I possess, the animals pay their tribute, but why does one woman refuse to bring her offering? Why does she cry in secret and stay at home when the whole world is out in gala attire. Behold, her hut is on the banks of the river near the great *pimpul* tree, and she belongs to the lowest class." At these words people ran excitedly towards the hut and drew the frightened woman out, saying:—"What virtue dost thou possess, woman, that the god notices thee and craves for thy offering?" and they were astonished to find her old, poor, and decrepit. She had scarcely anything in her house, only a turtle cooked without salt, and she said, "I did wish to offer something, and wept because I had nothing but this turtle. But I will lay it now before the god. If he has taken notice of me, blessed and happy I am though poor and old." She rose in haste and brought her simple offering on a plantain leaf. The multitude once more yelled out with a frantic yell and each laying hold of the ropes pulled a long and strong pull, and the car moved. The whole day it took to pass through the important street, and before the evening shadows fell it was drawn back into its usual place. Kamala was out with her friend Bhagirathi and others almost the whole day. She heard the cries of the multitude, saw the rush of the people and the waving mass of heads round her, and felt herself alone in the midst of the great crowd. She stood there caring not for it all. She had heard of such processions, and now that she had witnessed one with her own eyes the whole thing seemed unreal. Her mind was far away, following pictures of her own making. The might and power of the god whom the crowd was worshipping did not impress her as it did others, though she heard story after story regarding him. Bhagirathi told her that the car had stopped in the way once, when the *Pujaris* exclaimed that there was danger and that the deity was very angry and refused to move; and it was found that one of the seven runners in front of the car had dropped unconscious because he had unknowingly crossed the boundary line that separated one village from another. Then he was brought and laid before the car. The priests appealed to the deity and went three times round the car sprinkling holy water on the unconscious and apparently lifeless man, who rose and sat. Kamala heard all this and wondered, but somehow she felt that her God was not there. She thought of another scene, rude, bold, and grand that she had witnessed with her father—a mountainous place where in the midst of dim, dark surroundings, she experienced an exaltation of spirit which made her feel that God was there and that she was in the presence of an almighty power. How different was this scene? Her head ached, and she asked Bhagirathi wonderingly, "The gods are all that you say, but why do the demons have such power over human beings?"

"Demons? They are only the servants of the gods, soldiers that surround them. They are ferocious just as people are."

"But what about the demons that occupy groves, valleys, and tanks and possess people?" asked Kamala eagerly.

"Oh they are the spirits of the wicked who die, and they work harm to people, but they are cast out by spells. When the spell works the person possessed with the devil carries a huge stone which even four men cannot lift, and throws it out of the city gate. Thus the spirit is driven away. The spirits of good and virtuous persons become the *graha devas** which go straight to *swarga*,† only visiting the earth to foretell calamities, deaths, &c."

"I thought," said Kamala, "that the great God of the high hills and the level plains dwelt alone in his silent unapproachable abode, and cared not for the swarming multitudes of this world; that he only ruled the stars and the heavens, the storms and tempests, the floods and the broad flowing rivers; and that it was Fate that minded human affairs."

Bhagirathi laughed at this, and said with an air of confidence, "It is even so, but the gods of the hills are different; they are like the *sanyasis* among men." Poor Kamala did not understand all this, and she became more and more puzzled.

---

* Household gods. † Heaven.

CHAPTER X.

IN the evening the crowds began to disperse. Kamala saw men, women, and children struggling against the wind on the wide breezy plain on the way to their village homes. Her heart went out towards them. There was an elderly man in front of her with a basket swung behind him in which were snugly seated two children. A woman by him carried new pots on her head and a piece of sugarcane and a bunch of green vegetables in her hand. Her joy was great; the greens, which were a great luxury, were for the evening meal. The child that walked by her side tried to hold the end of the sugarcane and was delighted. But the journey was long and the child clutched at the sugarcane and said: "How far, mother?" Kamala's heart went out to the little girl and she thought of other little children in her hilly home whom she used to see under the trees and whom she would hush to sleep with melodies of her own making. Brought up in the innocent freedom of her mountain home she felt free like the air around her, and, untrammelled by caste superstition and fear, she entered joyously into the spirit of the rural diversions, taking an interest in the simple rustic souls around her, hugging their little black babies when they ran to her and joyously clung to her feet. She would forget to bathe after touching the Sudra and other low caste children, and no one found fault with the lovely *sanyasi's* daughter. But now how different everything was, how the artificial barriers of custom and caste separated her from all these people! What a contrast everything was! It took a long time for her to understand the meaning of the things that were open as daylight to her city bred sisters. They knew nothing of the freedom of hills and valleys and wide fields, the innocence and joy of country homes. Their precocious and artificial childhood ended in a premature and forced womanhood, and there were no gradations of feelings or thoughts for them. Just as the door of a city house leads abruptly into the street where everything is open and glaring, so the threshhold of their childhood opened suddenly into womanhood. Kamala often found it hard to realize things which the others took as a matter of course. The child who was walking in front of her had complained of cold, and the mother had put her *padur** over the child as a protection from the wind and had drawn her in a caressing way towards herself. Kamala felt that the child that she had just been pitying was rich indeed compared to herself, for where was her own mother? How she would have liked to walk by her side, free and happy, though going to a poor village hut!

As Kamala and Bhagirathi approached their homes they went to their favourite place on the river bank near a large clump of trees. The waters, interrupted by the entangled roots of trees, here formed numerous eddies and pools. "Come, come, Kamala," said Bhagi-

* The end of the upper cloth worn by women.

rathi, breathlessly, pulling her companion, who was dropping stones into the pool in front, "come behind this tree. I would not be seen here for all the world." They both tucked their *sarees* and hid themselves behind a huge tree. "Do you know who it is that is coming in this direction with your husband?" asked Bhagirathi excitedly. Kamala shook her head, and her heart beat wildly at the sight of her husband. Was she doing something wrong in hiding herself, she thought, and more than once she entreated Bhagirathi to let her go out.

"I won't budge an inch. I don't want your husband's companion to see me."

"Why, Bhagirathi, why? He is no relative of yours and if he were, he would not be angry at seeing us here."

Bhagirathi looked down into Kamala's eyes and said: "Don't you know why? Who told me that your husband had been visiting a person called Sai? It was he, Krishnan," and then clasping Kamala's hand to her bosom in a sudden paroxysm of grief she exclaimed: "Oh, Kamala, how can it be all nothing when I can't even tell you, my bosom friend, all that he has said to me?"

"*He* spoke to *you*?"

"Yes! Kamala. He had the audacity to do so, and in such terms, too. Ah! how can I tell you? Your innocence rebukes me. Enough! I shall have nothing to say to him. It is wrong, it *must* be wrong. Say you won't tell anyone."

"No! but why such ado?" said Kamala. "If he

is your relative you may speak to him. There is nothing wrong."

"Ah! Kamala! Do you know what he said? It is all due to my husband. The whole world knows that he cares not for me, and this man took the liberty of speaking to me. It was a place near the temple and he was behind a bush. Akabai was making her *poojah*, and the man gave me such a shock, for he came right up to me and thrust a letter into my hand." She took the letter out from her *choli** and showed it to Kamala, first looking all round to see that no one was observing them. "That night I could not sleep. What could I do? It was not my fault. Oh, I wish I could die. How I despise myself for all this. Don't look like that, Kamala. That night the thought came to me to run away with this man as he had proposed. He offered me his love. How guilty I feel now when I speak. I thought nothing of it then. I persuaded myself that it was natural for me to feel like that, and he said so in his letter. But I cannot write to him. I was so ashamed of it all in the morning and felt so angry with my husband, who by his conduct and treatment of me had given others a right to say such things to me. Then the revulsion of feeling would come now and then and I would say to myself, 'It would serve my husband right if I ran away.' The man had appointed this very spot for me to meet him, but I never went out of the house for a whole fortnight, and one day, Kamala, do you know, you were the means of

* The short-sleeved Jacket worn by Hindu women.

preserving me. I saw him accidentally alone, but I seemed to hear your voice. I was at the place where we generally meet when going to Kashi's house, near the bend of the road, and your voice gave me such a start that I turned away from the man and fled, saying you were coming. 'Who? - Ganesh's wife?' he asked. 'By the bye, I saw Ganesh at Sai's to-day.' This was said just to detain me. But the start your voice gave me seemed as it were to open my eyes. I felt I was doing a dreadful wrong by meeting that man there and I drew my *saree* over my face and walked quickly away with my water vessel tightly held in my hand. Akabai was just in front of me and I joined her, but my heart beat fast all the way and now I feel so afraid of myself, for my thoughts wander, oh! so much, and the words he used in his letter tempt me in my weak moments."

"Oh, Bhagirathi! This is dreadful. Let us burn this letter, and come away from this place. We don't want to see him, and don't let him again talk to you. Why, Bhagirathi, surely some medicine has been given to you to bewilder you. You must try *mantras* and charms to free you from this influence." And then turning round she saw the temple of Rohini in the distance, lit by the setting sun, and she clasped her hands and said: "Rohini *mata,** deliver my friend from this evil influence and I will make prostrations seven times seven on the great full moon day."

"Grant this prayer," said Bhagirathi, "and I will do so every month for one full year." And both

* Mother.

turned their faces towards the setting sun and bowed. As they were emerging from the grove Rukhma, the *sastri's* daughter, burst on them, starting them with a wild exclamation. "Here you are, I knew I should find you here. Did I not say that we couldn't do without one another? Three is the *Tirkut* and now we are four and that means devilry," for Harni had slipped in behind Rukhma. "It is a bewitched number, girls, and four would frighten anybody. There are three *apsaras*,* but what are four let me see."

"Stop your nonsense, you are always making up something or other," said Bhagirathi, shaking the dimpled, laughing girl. "With all your puranic reading in your house and your husband's coaching you are a little stupid monkey, let me tell you, with nothing but fun and laughter in your heart."

Rukhma pursed her lips and tried to look very dolorous, but changing her expression she said: "You need not think so now. There is something that I have got in my head that is really solid, for I have been thinking what is to be done. It is really getting unbearable, the way in which Harni's mother-in-law is going on. The poor girl has not been out to-day, and I have just now brought her from her grumbling reluctant mother-in-law."

The four girls formed a pretty contrast as they stood in the glow of the setting sun, the darkening grove behind them and the shining river flowing close by. Rukhma with her fat brown face, all dimples

* An imaginary being, a fairy.

and laughter, her eyes sparkling with fun, standing in the centre, the tall stately Bhagirathi in front, one hand resting on Kamala's shoulder and Kamala herself leaning on a stump of a tree close by, her soft fair face, looking softer and fairer in the evening light, and her dark dreamy eyes looking eagerly and wistfully now into one face, now into another, and Harni with her slight figure, her babyish face, sad and downcast, nestling by the side of Rukhma and holding one of her hands—the four formed a pretty picture. Rukhma was the only girl, besides Kashi, of Kamala's friends, who had a happy home, and she had a joyous buoyancy of manner. She could always twist a tale so as to make it ridiculous and excite laughter, and she herself was wont to indulge in a ringing laugh which was most contagious. "Come," she said, "mother-in-law is bad, that is a fact. What is to be done? Let us not make wry faces but put on a bold front—why can't we cheat Harni's mother-in-law and frighten her into good humour? I have a plan in view, if only you girls will listen to it. I can suggest a remedy for all your troubles, but we will take Harni's case first. The cranky old woman deserves it too!" Here Rukhma laughed loudly and added: "Oh, how I should like to see her thoroughly frightened and cowed down. She is so superstitious, too."

"But what is all this about, you mischiefmonger?" asked Bhagirathi.

"Wait! wait," said Rukhma, "Hear me. We shall represent three *apsaras** or witches or devils or what-

* An imaginary being, a fairy.

ever else you may call them—hair down, faces whitened, eyes flaming, dresses long with black stripes all over. The men will be away to-morrow till very late on account of the great fireworks *tamasha.** The back door of my house opens right by the side of Harni's yard, and we will pounce on the old woman as she comes out into the yard before retiring to bed, and if she screams we will frighten her more and escape. We will say: 'We are the three sisters of pestilence and we have come from the gods. We have witnessed the mental anguish and the *vanvasan*† of the poor suffering daughter-in-law and we will be revenged on her; and I will have my hair whitened to represent the eldest and most dreaded sister of cholera. I will wave my broomstick and my winnowing fan in her face, while you will merely point towards her and stay in the background and imitate the screeching of the owl just as I utter the words, 'I will be revenged.' Then you will slowly step back and disappear in the shadows and run home as fast as you can while I shall glide back waving my broomstick all the time. Let Harni go and sleep in her own place; so that when the old woman comes into the house gasping and frightened to death she may be ready there to sympathize with her. How I should like to see the old crone then.' At this she laughed another twittering laugh and said: "Come, girls, don't you see the fun? Why do you demur?"

"The fun we see," said Bhagirathi, "but who is to bear the beating afterwards? We are sure to be discovered."

* Entertainment. † Fasting.

"Beating! Pha! who will find us out? It will be such a lesson to the old tyrant who is sure to tell others of the visitation, and then the confidential whispers that will follow—Ha! Ha! Ha!—and the women gathering mysteriously around her, and the shaking of their wise heads—I see it all before me. Won't there be fun? Harni will at least be free for a full year, I tell you."

"Oh, no!" exclaimed Harni, who was listening with a solemn face and dilated eyes. "They are sure to put the blame of the whole visitation on me and my poor husband." Hereupon the three girls shook the poor frightened Harni and laughed loudly. Thus ended in smoke Rukhma's wild plan.

CHAPTER XI.

IT was a garden house in Sivagunga that was rented by Kashi's father for the occasion of Gungi's wedding. A party was given by the *shastri* in honour of his daughter's marriage, and women celebrated for their singing were specially invited to it from Rampur and other places. A large number of people were invited to this singing party without reference to caste or creed, and among those present was Sai.

It was midnight and the moon was full. The shadows waved ominously under the mango trees in the garden. A woman was seen in the midst of the flitting lights and shadows sitting on a large stone and talking eagerly to a man who stood by her. From the house came the hubbub of many voices. The cymbals were sounding, but above all was heard the high trilling melody of a female voice accompanied on the *veena*.* "Well, this is a good opportunity for us to meet"—it was Ramabai's husband who was speaking to Sai in the garden—"the gods are more favourable now. How did your visit to Ganesh end that day? I knew that the house would be full of people and that few would know who came and who went away. Hence it was I sent you to Ganesh that day." She was about to interrupt him, but he stopped her, saying, "Wait! Wait! Let me be open with you.

* A Hindu musical instrument.

I meant this visit of yours to have a double effect :— that Kamala should see you with her husband accidentally and that her jealousy should be aroused. I told him that all women are of a low, jealous nature, at which he was very indignant. It is so provoking the stupid way he treats her, as if there were nobody else that could compare with her in beauty and other qualities. I also want Kamala to know what she has to fear in you." It was with difficulty he stopped Sai from interrupting him, and now she exclaimed with considerable irritation, "She fear me? why, she looked at me as if the very sight of me were pollution. The impertinent hussy! and the look of triumph that she cast on me when she said, 'Ganesh is not here! He is gone for a couple of days,' as much as to say that *he* could not be aware of my coming there and that there could be no engagement between us. I felt—well I won't say what I felt. I should like to see that man at my feet just to revenge myself on her, though I did not like your sending me there without knowing his whereabouts. She put on the air of a princess, the penniless brat, as she pointed to her husband's room, and walked straight through the hall not deigning to look back on me."

"Well, never mind," said Ramabai's husband, laughing. "I am glad you saw her, and that you dislike her," and then followed a whispered conversation between the two, after which Sai burst out laughing, and said: "Oh! I see you want Ganesh to marry that rich and highly connected girl in Rampur and want to use me as a tool to drive away

Kamala. But the plan you mention won't do. Merely maligning her character when she goes off in a huff to her father's house won't keep her away for ever. Of course people may believe that a *sanyasi's* daughter cannot be trusted, as the wandering, restless element is in her blood, and may not be surprised to learn that she had proved a failure. Kamala is herself proud enough to keep away from her husband's house when she hears such things spoken of her, but Ganesh won't be satisfied. However, I know of something else, which if true, will serve your purpose better, but of that I shall tell you afterwards."

Portions of this conversation were being listened to from a window overlooking the garden, for Sai was an interesting personage to many women, and her movements were carefully watched.

Some weeks after Gungi's marriage Kamala had the pleasure of seeing Kashi in her own house. There was a ceremony in the house and the *shastri's* wife was asked to bring Kamala with her. The two girls had not met for a long time, and they rejoiced to see each other. At the first opportunity they could get they went hand in hand into the backyard for a long chat. It was evening and the dewy atmosphere was laden with the scent of the *mogra* and *champa* flowers. Many a thing had happened in Kamala's house since the two friends last met. Kashi had heard of gay doings and was anxious to know everything. Kamala, after telling her all she could about Gungi's marriage, had to answer a number of questions relating to her husband, which she did shyly, hiding her face on

Kashi's shoulder. "Oh, he is so good," said Kamala, "but so many things have happened lately that I am afraid, Kashi, that he may change. He is all that I can wish when he is alone with me, but somehow I feel that he despises me when others are present. He is not his usual self then. He has now almost given up teaching me and lately—Oh, I don't know how to tell it to you—I have been so troubled." Here Kamala paused, and then, seeing the eager look in Kashi's eyes, tried to explain all. "You know," she began again, "that Gungi's wedding took place a week ago. Some days before the event active preparations were being made for the marriage. The house your father lent was full of guests and we had to find accommodation for some of them in sheds erected in the garden. Many people were coming and going, and one day whom should I see coming straight towards our room, but a woman whose name I afterwards learned was Sai."

"Sai Zadhovini?" said Kashi in astonishment.

"Yes! I did not know then who she was. I took her for one of the guests or visitors. The bold woman only laughed in my face at my confusion and asked me where my husband was. I was surprised at this question, but further on when she spoke to me my heart sank within me. She looked so beautiful and bewitching. What could she want with my husband, I thought to myself? But one thing, Kashi, made me almost leap with joy. She knew not my husband's movements. So it was not by appointment that she had come, and I could not help giving expression to my feelings. To me the very sight of her was pollution, and I turned to go away. But oh, Kashi, her parting look sent a throb of fear through me. It seemed to convey a threat, and this is what disturbs me most now. I care not how much persecution I undergo at home. The people are after all my husband's own people and they are good to him though they may hate me. But ah! I shudder at the thought of this woman. Do you think, Kashi, that she will come between him and me? At times this thought does not distract me and I try to feel resigned, but to lose a friend, the only one in my husband's home, the thought of this is sometimes unbearable. At the same time, Kashi, when my husband appears cold and does not keep his word to me, I feel the old indifference to all my surroundings come over me. I work, work, work, to drown all thought, and the hardest and the worst kind of work is to me the most welcome. Tell me, Kashi, what I ought to do." Kamala held her friend's hands tight as if in an iron grasp and burst into tears, adding: "Oh! I wish I could stay with you always."

Kashi put her hand round Kamala and pressed her towards herself and said after a long silence: "Oh, Kamala, I know Sai, but who could have sent her to your husband? Be sure that somebody is trying to ruin you, my lotus flower. Be careful. The gods alone can protect you."

Kamala was startled by Kashi's words. "Do you think that somebody did really send her to him?" she asked.

"Sure as anything," said Kashi. "She is a dangerous woman. She has the wiles of the devil and is very influential, though she is not so degraded as the ordinary sort of women of her kind, and that is why I am so afraid of her. Did your mother-in-law see her? Did she stay in the house?" Kamala shook her head and said she did not know, for many *pandals* had been erected in the garden to accommodate guests.

Just then Bhagirathi, who had overheard the latter part of the conversation, joined them, and all three walked towards the river.

"But who is this Sai? Who could have sent her to my husband?" asked Kamala again, dreamily looking over the long line of trees by the side of the river.

"Who else could have sent her to your husband but your husband's people?" said Bhagirathi vehemently. "It is they that work all the harm for us. O Kamala, there are many things that we could tell, but our mouths are shut. They think that we cannot feel. They benumb us by giving us work that takes the strength out of us. We get disgusted with life. The daily drudgery, the murmuring and grumbling leave nothing behind that we can desire, but we are thankful for even a little sunshine such as this—this liberty to see our friends and take a walk outside our prisons."

Bhagirathi was a tall girl with an oval face of a soft subdued bronze-like colour, to which the light of her flushing dark eyes gave a lovely glow. Her figure was slim and she tossed her head and turned about with scornful gestures. Yet so graceful were her movements that one would have thought that she was the queen of some unknown gypsy realm come to take vengeance on those around her. Her language was always vehement, and, poor girl, she had reason to be bitter. How much reason, others could scarcely understand. Her girl friends knew and sympathised with her, impetuous and fiery as she was, and there never was a friend more sincere than she. She would have given her life, if need be, for those who were kind to her. Both Kashi and Kamala listened to Bhagirathi's words calmly. The girls were nearing the river on the banks of which just in front of them were temples and groves and beyond a huge vast plain. "Hush! we must not talk here," said Bhagirathi, and changed the conversation abruptly. "There, do you see those groves? The priests live there, and there is the temple opposite. Come, let us lay our flowers before the goddess Rohini Mata, *she* knows everything, the black and the white, she sees all. 'Wherever there is a ditch the water will stand.' Why need we talk? My mind is clear as the rocky pool, you can see for yourself. I keep no grudge, though I speak harshly and fly into a temper."

"But really, Bhagirathi, did you hear anything?" asked Kamala.

"Did I hear? Who brings trouble and discontent into a family, if it is not the mother-in-law? Did not mine do the same for a long time, till my husband got quite disgusted with me and took to somebody else.

Of course now I am the firebrand. I cannot be touched or spoken to. I fly at them, why? because my heart is so sore. It burns and burns. What is the use of wealth and plenty? My mother-in-law looks at me with a smile of triumph as if to say:—'Look, oh! you self-willed creature. See what your conduct has brought you to. What was the use of your struggling for independence? You have got it now, but why do you writhe with pain and fly into a rage when spoken to?'" These words Bhagirathi uttered with considerable vehemence, but afterwards turning to Kamala she said softly: "One thing, Kamala, I warn you against. Be careful about Ramabai's husband. I was anxious to see Sai and watched her through the window on the day of the singing party, and heard Ramabai's husband say something to Sai which appeared suspicious, for I heard your name pronounced now and then in some sentences which I could not understand. But come, girls, there is the goddess Rohini. It is getting dark, the bells are ringing. The priests are out with their censers and the lights are lit. Come, let us walk by the side of the road. Don't fall in the way of the advancing gods. You know it is just the time when they take their evening walks."

Boom! Boom! the sounds come from the temple. The *Mata* has left the temple. The bells ring loudly. People from all parts are hastening to the temple, some with brass plates full of flowers, others with offerings of different things to be laid before the goddess. At a certain place in front of the temple they bow, a change in the music intimates to them that the goddess is standing at the doorway, and they murmur their petitions to her and prostrate themselves nine times, and then, advancing, take the holy ashes, the *basil* leaves, and go round the temple three times before leaving the place. Not a word is uttered by the people during the *poojah.* Fear and trembling fill their hearts. Some break cocoanuts, some burn camphor for sick people, and some count beads for merit. In the dark groves near by are seen the hideous figures of the *bhairagis* and priests, huge, big-built men with coarse features begrimed with ashes. The girls clasp each other's hands as they behold these men, who stare at them with a coarse, rude stare.

"Oh, Kashi," said Kamala, "I feel so afraid of these men. One comes to beg food, and when I give him anything he offers a blessing, but he does look so dreadful."

"They have a power in their eyes, it is said," remarked Kashi. "Have you heard of people following them and being entirely at their mercy? They can do anything they wish, it seems."

"Oh, how dreadful," said Kamala. "How I dislike the priest that comes to our house. He has always something to say about me, and I try to hide myself from him, but he finds me out. Something or other is needed for the *poojah,* and I have to take it to him and he watches me so minutely that I feel frightened. Do you think he knows I dislike him?"

"They know everything," said Bhagirathi. "Their gods tell them everything while they are in a trance, and they have even power over the gods. Some of the bad ones go even so far as to order their gods. They get so skilful in their *mantras* and so powerful. The *poojaree* of this temple before the present one was a most wicked person. Have you heard how he died? Well, our goddess Rohini is a good married woman. You know the story of how she preserved our city from being washed away. When the floods came in the night and the *bunds* were in danger, it was she who went to the *mamlatdar,* roused him from sleep, and told him to bring his workmen. And when he demurred and said : 'Oh ! it is impossible to secure the *bunds* in one night,' she frowned on him and said : 'Come, as many of you as can, and each one bring a spadeful of sand. I will see to the rest. Do you know who I am ?' That night they worked as they never did before, and the city was saved. Well, Rohini is a virtuous woman and used to be very indignant at the liberties this priest took with her. Once at midnight, the time when she generally went out on her rounds to watch the city, this man came swinging along under the influence of *bhang.* She had just left the temple and was in the yard, but he did not notice her and walked right in and called out loudly : 'Halloa ! wench, come out.' This was very rude, for the term used could only apply to a concubine or a dancing girl. The goddess heard it and turned round in a rage. She was free in the air and no more under his power, and she gave him such a slap on the back that he fell down, spat blood, and died. There is no trifling with her. She requires clean men with good hearts, not those that stare at women and use bad words. Her virtue is very great. By the power of it she goes dry over waters and floods, and that is why women sing to her when grinding the corn :—

> 'The front springs dry
> And the back springs gush out
> At the feet of Rohini,
> Our lovely Rohini,
> The Rohini who presides
> Over the banks of the river.'"

Kamala in her turn approached the temple with her heart full of misgivings. She had an indescribable yearning to pour out her mind to the great and good goddess, Rohini. She prostrated herself in front of the temple. Her prayer was the dumb cry of the heart for a God to rule where no order appeared to exist, and to give strength and support in the midst of struggle and strife. A blind fate, *Vithi*, appeared to direct all. "O God," exclaimed Kamala, as she prostrated herself before the hideous images, and the wind moaned in the trees and seemed to prolong the sorrowful note, "O God, if thou art present here"—and a shudder came over her as she thought of the evils that were being planned and that loomed before her. But with this came a more consoling thought. As she dreamily looked at the long stretch of road that led to her home, the mound by its side, and the curve at the far end, she seemed to feel that her God was not far off, and that He was able to help her. Her heart rose as she looked over all and unconsciously added: "Yes, Thou art here. Thou knowest me. Thou hast made me and lookest on all. Thou seest the wicked and the good. The vile plots of the wicked thwart. Rescue my husband and me. The false is around me everywhere. I invoke thy aid and supplicate thy help." The winds roared and rushed and the trees shook ominously. It was to her an awful moment. She thought that her prayer perhaps was too daring and that the god was walking in the twilight in the unseen elements. Perhaps he was approaching her. She fell on her face once more. The loud mournful sound of the roaring, rushing wind passed away and there was a hush. Would anything happen to her for her daring? Would the deity before her get angry and strike her dead? Her hands were clasped in prayer and her mind was concentrated to the uttermost. Just then the voice of her husband fell on her ears, but when she lifted her head she saw another face which gave her a dreadful start. Her husband was by her side and was telling her something, but she could not catch the meaning of the words, for the eyes of the other man had transfixed her. "That man! oh, that man! why does he come?" and she pressed her heart as she walked by the side of her husband. The person in front was no other than the young physician who had cured her, and whom she had met under strange circumstances at Dudhasthal. The gaze was unmistakable and she wondered at its power. But her husband led her to Kashi, saying, "Be prepared to go soon to your father." Then Kamala awoke as it were from a dream and asked, "Why? What?" Her husband smiled, and looking into her confused face, asked her if she was bewitched in the holy grove, and said: "Have you not heard what I have been saying to you all this time? Your father wants you. He is ill. Come home at once and prepare to go."

Ganesh's nature was hard to comprehend. He had many good impulses but he was indolent, and there was a selfish element in his character. Everything was subservient to his pleasure, and it is no wonder that he regarded Kamala as a sort of a chattel made to give him pleasure and minister to his wants. He seemed not to be aware of any pain that he caused by his coldness and indifference towards her. She was his wife, his property, and he felt that there was no need for him to exert himself to draw her nearer to himself. He did not trouble in the least as to what she was doing so long as his own hours were spent in pleasure. He was intensely kind to her when he was with her, for it gave him pleasure to be kind and to see the beaming look of gratitude in her face. He was a man who could not bear to see outward signs of pain or sorrow, and he tried to shirk displeasing duties just to avoid the pain and trouble of them. Intelligent conversation gave him pleasure and his mother's company satisfied his vanity, for he was the pet son. Ramabai's husband, who had studied Ganesh's character very carefully, tried his best to bring Sai more and more in contact with him. There was a charm in Sai's company. Her intelligent repartee, her jovial, humorous way of taking off people, her wide knowledge of the world, and her scathing ridicule of those who did not fall in with her way of thinking, could not but attract Ganesh towards her. Kamala did not realize the weak side of her husband's character. She was herself a sensitive, high-souled girl, and she only looked at the bright side of those around her. Her own heart was quite unselfish, and entirely devoted to those for whom she felt any regard. Latterly Ganesh felt a certain constraint in Kamala's presence, for he could not always manufacture excuses for not keeping his many promises to teach her. He felt rebuked at the sight of the light which leapt in Kamala's eyes and the flash of pleasure on her face at his approach; and he was conscious that her nature was higher than his own and felt uncomfortable. He was even angry with himself for having at first made such determined efforts to teach her, and for having led her to expect so much notice and attention from him.

CHAPTER XII.

SAI'S coming was a great diversion. She was seen everywhere and continually spoken of by the young men of his company. They congratulated him on the notice she took of him in public, and he was very much pleased. Poor Kamala felt very much disturbed in her mind as her acquaintances spoke to her of having seen her husband in Sai's company, and the news of her father's illness caused her additional anxiety of another kind. Now she feared for Ganesh and now for her father and her mind was distracted. "If anything happen to my husband," she said to herself after a great deal of thought, "it won't be through any fault of mine. If he commits any mistakes or comes under this woman's power what can I do? The threads of destiny are taken out of my hands by a Higher power. My father requires me. Yet something tells me I am needed by my husband too." In her difficulty she muttered some kind of prayer to the temple gods, though she felt that it was of little use. In her concern for her husband she had sought to repress her affection for her father, but having learned of his illness she could restrain it no longer, and casting herself down on the ground she wept, crying, "O my father, my father. I am here and who is there to help you?" The thought that perhaps he would die before she could see him made her intensely miserable, and she could not sleep the whole night.

Next morning she had to go with her mother-in-law to her mountain home which she had not seen for so long a time. Ganesh was up early. He had slept soundly, little thinking of Kamala's troubles, but when he saw her red swollen eyes and downcast face and her vain attempts to quiet herself by bustling about, his conscience smote him. She was constantly going to the outer door and back, restlessly waiting for her mother-in-law to come out of her room. Ganesh saw all this and could not help going near her and saying to her: "Don't cry." She drew back at these words, for the tears began to gush from her eyes and she went to a side room to hide them. Ganesh followed, and lifted her drooping covered face, saying: "No! No! Kamala. Don't go on like that." Something like pity filled his heart and the thought of his neglect of her all these days flashed across his mind. It was somehow painfully mingled with fear at her going away. A vague feeling as if he would lose her came over him. But he shook away the thought and laughed uneasily and said: "Kamala, you are a little baby to cry so. Your father is not so bad. I made special inquiries of Ramachunder Rao yesterday, and he said that your father was only pining to see you. No wonder! He has not seen you for so long." Then, hearing voices near, he hastily drew away his hand and said in a whisper: "I shall come to see you soon, and now go."

Kamala's thoughts on the way were fixed on the home far in front of her on the top of the distant hill. Her head was reeling, and a feeling of unreality came over her. She passed the bazaar street at the other end of the town—the street that she had so often crossed with her father in those bygone days when she was carried on his back, and she felt a choking in her throat at the thought of those visits. Ah! where was the caressing hand, the dear voice calling her to go to sleep and not to mind anything? The rice fields waved as of old, dimpling with every breath of wind, and she remembered her old joy when she and her father waded through them; and she looked up wondering whether the sunlight was still there and the wind, her old play fellow: and she saw the morning rays struggling with the soft mist under the trees and lighting up the shining leaves and the dew-laden tops of the trees. Then she thought of the long years that had passed since she was last there and the change that had come on her, and she exclaimed to herself: "Oh, where are all the old joys? Will they never come back to me any more?" and she shuddered at the thought. Nearer the hill Kamala's mother-in-law told her to run on, for she had been so eager to go forward. On the hill Kamala saw her old friend Yeshi approaching. Her heart stood still. "Yeshi," she said, and realized for the first time the great change that had come over her, for Yeshi held a child in her arms. But there was no time for words. Blame not the girl because she stumbled into Yeshi's arms—her own beloved Yeshi—and cried. There was no room for the pride of caste, for the touch-me-not feelings of the Brahman all vanished before the gush of her old affection. Yeshi held her mistress in her arms, delighted, surprised, and was almost lost for joy. "Kamalabai, how changed you are!" she said.

"How is my father?" asked Kamala, eagerly.

"Your father was very ill, but he is better. Don't be anxious. I have been looking out for you." And they both went up hand in hand to the old home, Kamala stumbling at every stone and ready to fall.

Eagerly entering the hut she fell on her father's bed: "Father! father! Oh, how I have longed to see you." The suppressed feelings of years gave way, and sobs—heavy deep sobs—came from her.

"Kamala! Kamala dear! let me see you," said the feeble old man, as he raised her head and kissed her. The sobs were hushed, and a great peacefulness stole over her as if she had found her haven of rest at last. She did not ask him any questions. She gave him one inquiring look and laid her head on his bosom while he held her tight, looking into her eyes and caressing her. Thus she lay when her mother-in-law entered the room, but she moved not. "What, Kamala?" said the old dame, and then seeing that she did not move asked: "Is the girl sleeping?"

"No! let her be thus," said the old *sanyasi*, in his feeble voice. "It is a great thing for me to have her near. In her childhood we were never separated."

Meanwhile Kamala sank motionless from sheer exhaustion, and she was allowed to remain beside her father.

* * * *

It was a dark, primeval forest. The deep, solemn stillness was broken only by the constant falling of dead leaves, which, collected in heaps below, lay in some places to a depth of three or four feet. The leaves one by one rustled and fell with a perceptible thud through the length and breadth of the forest. The huge gigantic trees, covered with creepers, met overhead, their branches intertwining and forming a huge canopy, beneath which the sunlight rarely penetrated, the light of day paling into a soft greyish blue twilight. The forest lay on a high plateau among weird, bleak hills, which were unattractive even to birds and beasts. When the mists came curling up from the valleys or descended from the hills they wrapped the forest in their soft white fleecy arms and settled on the tree-tops, giving to the whole scene a dim shadowy appearance, as if it was a phantom forest waving in cloudland far far away. But when the cold winds rushed from the hill-tops they roared and crashed through the branches, and the noise of the awakened forest resembled that of the ocean when in its fury it breaks on some rock-bound coast.

Such was the forest of *Panabaras*, the abode of the far-famed sage, Aranyadaya, who was learned in all the old Vedic and Puranic lore, and who was regarded by people, who had heard of his fame but had not seen him, as possessing the key to the healing art. The sage loved to have his abode here where he could gather rare herbs and enjoy the sanctity of seclusion. He had devoted his whole life to study and meditation and only a favoured few had the privilege of his personal acquaintance. Among these were Narayen, the *saniyasi*, and the young physician, Ramchander.

The *Rishi* was seated on a mat under a huge tree a little away from his solitary hut and Ramchander was by his side. After some moments of silence he called out softly: "Ramchander!"

"Guru Raj!" said the young man, reverently, "Speak, I am listening."

"My days are nearly over, Ramchander, though it seems as if my friend Narayen will go before me. Have you grasped everything I have told you? Do you think you will be able to keep the torch of knowledge burning when we are gone?"

"I will try, my master, ignorant and unlearned as I am." Saying this, Ramchander, the young disciple, approached the sage so as to listen further to his instructions; but the mood for talking had passed away and the old man seemed absent. After some time Ramchander said: "I have bad news to tell you." But even this did not seem to have any effect on the old man. Then after a further interval Ramchander continued: "I have read all the *Charmapatrikas* (parchments) you asked me to read. I have found the serpentine root that is so rare. I have found it in the cliffs youder, a solitary clinging herb. The plates, platters and powders are ready." But all this was said in vain, for the great *rishi* was lost in thought. Nothing could awaken him from his dreamy reverie. He was evidently deep in thought, and he rose and walked as a blind man would, feeling for the trunks of trees and looking intently on the ground, as if trying to catch sounds unheard by other ears. The young man waited, for he knew his master's moods.

At last the sage turned sharply and grasping Ramchander's arm shook him in excitement and said in a hoarse whisper: "I have been hearing the sound of waters. There is a spring hidden here somewhere and I have been calling to mind the pages in the sacred book that refer to this spring. It is the famous spring of *Ashtarini* that we read of in the old books. Haste, search for it, lest I lose the sound again. Go straight on and turn to the left. There you will see a rock. Near by must be the rude image of *Vanadeva* covered over all these years with dead leaves Feel with this stick; close to the image must be the medicinal spring whose waters give health and life. It bubbles up and you must be careful to open its mouth and let the waters run out. Haste! something tells me that my friend Narayen sorely needs our aid."

"Yes, I came to tell you that he was lying in a deep faint."

"Well, be quick! Fetch the water and we shall go in."

Ramachander did as he was told. He found the bubbling spring. Then he and the old sage went to their primitive hut of leaves where they found Narayen lying on a mat. The music of the forest was heard around the hut in all its grandeur, but Narayen seemed to be unconscious of it. The *rishi* approached, felt his pluse, and waking him made him drink some water from the famous spring.

"You have sacrificed much, my friend, to gain knowledge and its power," said the *rishi* to Narayen, "and now you must not despair. What are your wishes?"

"My wishes?" said Narayen, in a soft whisper; "I have only one. I wish to pass away quietly in this great temple of leaves but my heart longs to see my girl. Then I should like to die peacefully."

"But, father," said Ramchander, "it is not possible to bring her here. Let me take you back to your old home in Anjinighur. You must not despair, you have drunk of the waters of healing and you shall not die yet."

Thus was Narayen, the *saniyasi*, brought over to Anjinighur, where his old home was, and Kamala was sent for. Since Kamala's marriage the old man had led a solitary life He was absorbed chiefly in abstract thought. His mind was puzzled over many things. He felt the unreality of everything that appealed to the senses. All things were changing and yet there remained something eternal and unchangeable and that was God. But what was the sensible material universe? Was it an emblem of the deity? If so how could it partake of the nature of the changeable? Or was it a part of the deity? What were the *Shastras* for:—the endless ritual and symbol worship contained in them, if God was everywhere and in everything? Surely in human beings He was manifest. Such were some of the *saniyasi's* thoughts. He felt that he had no scope for such speculations except in solitude, apart from the world. There alone the highest emotions of his soul were called forth, there he felt the greatest exaltation of spirit, and there he heard the voice of God speaking to his soul direct. His one object was to become absorbed in the deity and to become one with Him, and for this he found it necessary to suppress all the passions of the senses. He was very fond of the company of his *rishi* friend, Aranyadaya, and when any thought troubled him he went to the old sage for advice and counsel. Often Narayen would emerge from his solitude inspired with a mission and with enthusiasm expound to the people the real meaning of the *Shastras*. He would grow so eloquent and yet remain so practical in his eloquence that people wondered at the great knowledge of the world and of mankind that he possessed.

It is your old religion, he would say, the religion of your ancient *rishis* and sages. Leave it not, change it not for any other. God is God under whatever name you worship Him. You take His different attributes and erect temples as symbols of these different attributes and worship them separately. That is well; but He is not in the hills nor in the green waving trees, and yet He is there and everywhere. You hear His voice but you cannot see Him. He is a part of everything you see. Now He is chaste Rohini; now the protecting Bhagvani; now the guardian deity that sustains you. To the wicked He is a fierce demon, till proper propitiation is made in the way of sacrifices and the passions are subdued; but to higher natures is given the privilege of being absorbed in the deity. Do not care for pleasures, for pleasures are a delusion. Work out your salvation by deeds of merit and acts of charity. Thus Narayen would discourse, argue, and talk, now sitting on the steps of a temple, now on a river ghaut, and now in the grove of the *shastris;* and he was known and reverenced by all.

The intense love of the Indian for a life of solitude and meditation has been a puzzle to foreigners, who forget that a keen sensibility is one of the marked characteristics of the Hindu mind. The Hindu is subject to moments of depression and exaltation of spirits, and is deeply affected by intense spiritual cravings which are generally alien to men of other climes. He loves meditation because he finds a deep pleasure in it, and he hugs to himself the new found joys of the intellect, and would sacrifice anything to satisfy the longings of an awakened soul. He leaves the world and the petty worries of life because they come between him and his life of meditation, and he resorts to places where he can be free and enjoy to his heart's content the pleasures of the soul in the contemplation of all that is good and beautiful. He does not find it dull to live alone, for he enjoys pleasures of which men sensually inclined know nothing. His wants are few and easily satisfied, and his love of all that is beautiful in nature is great. The wind blows a cool, refreshing breeze and he experiences the keenest pleasure from it. The clouds form on the hills, arrayed in gorgeous colours, and he looks at them, at the gaily decked flowers, at the milky cascades, at the warbling brooks, and at the merry birds, and feels he has companions in them all. The mountain goats, the cows and their calves, and the very crows gather round the recluse and in numerous delightful trusting ways proclaim him their friend; and they weary him not as human friends do. He leaves them when he chooses, changes his abode, or goes on a pilgrimage to sacred spots, always returning to his solitude when he is inclined. Others know nothing of the luxury of such a life.

CHAPTER XIII.

WHEN Narayen was brought to Anjinighur, Ramchander hastened to take the message to Kamala's husband and returned immediately. He was in the hut when Kamala entered, for he had nursed Narayen through the night. But Kamala saw him not, and as soon as she entered, Ramchander left the place. He stayed in the temple precincts that day, but he was unable to stay longer at Anjinighur, as important messages had come for him and for Narayen, asking them to go at once to Sinhagud, and Narayen urged Ramchander to go and not to mind him. The young man had to pass over the ghauts through one of the important passes to get to Sinhagud where his mother was lying dangerously ill.

It was a weird mountain scene that he witnessed as the path led him down through rugged ravines on the side of a precipitous hill. Lower down, the tangled branches met overhead and huge rocks stood perpendicularly on each side. Streams gushed forth at various points, their noise filling the whole valley. Ramchander, who was on horseback, went slowly, the sure-footed animal guiding him cautiously over rocks and stones. The mid-day heat was great, and once an uncanny sensation crept over him as he thought he saw, in a dark grove close by, a hideous red image of Kali, and two eyes, bright like living coals, peering at him from behind. But the feeling vanished as he left the spot. The animal stopped to drink by the way, and Ramchander looked around when he reached the deep valley. It was a scene of great beauty. Huge tree ferns, hill plantains, and rushing brooks appeared on all sides, and light-leaved trees shed their yellow bloom on all. "Oh! who would think that this place, where everything looks so lovely, is the dreaded Sadashiva Dholl, in which robberies and murders have been committed? The stones tell no tales." So thought Ramchander as he looked around. A huge mountain now rose on either side, and a ledge of rock projected from one of them right overhead. "What a nice place to sit and dream. Yes, it has all been dreaming with me. I could never go through the devotions like the others. The lovely light on the hills, the birds, the gurgling rills all have distracted my attention, and when the clouds have come rolling down like feathery fleeces, covering all up in their soft white arms I have walked up the mountain heights to see the effect on the valley below; and the flashing lightning and the rolling thunder have made me dance with joy. In my exultation I have cried to God—the great God—and my utmost soul I have poured forth in His praise." With such thoughts in his mind Ramchander passed through the narrow defile and entered a broad smiling valley; and as the mountains receded, his horse gave a neigh of pleasure. Just then a figure on horseback emerged from the hills, and it came alongside of him from behind. It made him start, but when he found that the rider was a woman he smiled at his fears. The woman was sitting astride a small pony. She was small built, thin and wiry, and wonderfully bright in appearance. Her dark eyes sparkled with intelligence and her small oval face was eagerly turned towards the passer. There was a grace and tact in her movements as she directed her pony over rough stones and steep places. She had not what one would call a fair colour, but she looked striking in her purple, heavy-laced *saree* and light brown complexion.

"We are well out of it, are we not?" she said, coming along-side of Ramchander. But he said not a word, only gave her a look. "My attendants are behind and they will be breathless with running, for they did not expect me to go so fast," she said.

Ramchander smiled at her eagerness to make him talk. He had seen her before, but he feigned not to know her and said: "Have you far to go?"

"Just to yonder village. But the sun is high and I need not fear. You will guide me. There is another dark pass yet to go through. I think I saw you in Sivagunga, but you change your garb so; nobody can make you out."

"How do you know that?" asked Ramchander, looking at her curiously.

"Leave Sai not to know anything."

"And you are Sai?"

"Yes. Who did you think I was?" said she, with a loud laugh. "Nothing is kept secret from me. I know you better than you imagine, and you are in my power just now, but don't fear. Sai does no harm to those whom she likes."

"And those were your *Bheels* that I saw watching me yonder from over these rocks?"

"Hush! don't tell anyone. I like to be open with those who are my friends."

"And, pray, tell me who I am?"

"You are Ramchander Row, the nephew of Narayen, the *sanayasi*," she said, watching his face minutely. He gave a slight start, at which she laughed and said: "You thought you could hide that. And Kamalabai, our great beauty, was once betrothed to you, was she not?" At this Ramchander visibly changed. He threw off his reserve and turning to her said in a frank, jovial way: "I won't tell you how far you are right, but we can keep secrets, can't we? you mine and I yours." "All right," she said, laughing, "that is our first compact. And now you promise to pay a visit to our village. There is a nice *dharmashala** where you will be comfortable, and I will see that your men are all provided for." She knew she had gained a victory and that through Kamala. Her woman's instinct told her that there was more to follow; and hazarding a guess, she asked: "Were you not at Dudhasthal?"

"I may or may not have been," he said evasively, but laughed as he looked into her eyes, for evidently she was feeling his mind.

"And you are still sweet on the girl. You have not yet forgiven her marriage which the old dotard her father stupidly hurried through," she said sarcastically, glad to find confirmation now of every guess of

* A resting place for travellers.

hers in the slight changes that she saw in his face and behaviour.

At her last words Ramchander laughed, though she expected him to be angry. "What a woman you are!" he said, after the hearty laugh which had taken her aback. "Don't you know when once married she is out of one's reach? I wish her well and not for the whole world would I wish her happiness to be marred. I don't like your talking in this light fashion about another man's wife. She knows not our relationship."

"And yet she walks with you," said Sai with a loud laugh, meant to conceal her anxiety, for this was a bold guess founded on the first. She fancied she had seen Ramchander or somebody like him, from a distance, guiding Kamala through the crowd at Dudhasthal, and she watched him minutely now, to see whether she was right. The words startled him not a little and the laugh sounded coarse in Ramchander's ears. He felt as if he had received a rough slap, and he bit his lips and repented of having opened his mind and given her reason to talk so. He looked at her absently for a minute, however, before speaking, and said quite calmly: "You know the whole relationship now, but you are to keep it to yourself. Kamala is quite innocent, and after her father I am her guardian." What Sai's long tongue would do he knew not, and he was frightened. Never did the little incident at Dudhasthal appear so serious in his eyes as on that occasion.

"Oh, is it so?" said Sai, trying to speak quite indifferently. She had seen the change and had said to herself: "He won't stop in my village even after my asking him to do so, but Kamala is in my hands now. I see my way clearly." Then after a pause she said to Ramchander loudly, "Come, Rao Saheb, don't be displeased, halt in our village. I have nothing to say against the poor dear soul, I only happen to know some of her relations and thought I saw her at Dudhasthal, where I went to learn some *ragas,* for there were great and learned musicians expected there, and the three great *ragas* (famed classical pieces of music) were to be played, and we women have to live by our art. I take care to improve myself on all occasions."

Ramchander listened to Sai's humble confessions, and was more puzzled than before. After all he decided to stay in the village and not give offence, for he felt he was somehow in her power.

* * * *

Kamala's going to her father's house was the subject of a great deal of gossip and speculation on the part of her friends at Sivagunga. Four or five women were sitting together in an inside room opening into the inner quadrangle of Bhagirathi's house. Before them was the betel leaf tray, which also contained the favourite jessamine flowers woven into garlands. On another plate were placed the sandal paste and attar oil in silver vessels. The women were seated on mats and were chewing betel nut. The widows, with their *sarees* covering their shaven heads, stood near by, some leaning on the walls and others holding on to half open doors. They did not do much of the talking, though they smiled and now and then put in some pithy remarks. One old widow, however, demanded much attention as she sat a little away from the others reclining on a long cushion.

"How strange," said one of the married women, "that the *shastri's* door is now quite shut to the street and nobody seems to go in and out."

"Perhaps they have all gone somewhere," said a fair fat woman with her mouth full of betel nut. "I hate that woman Ramabai," she said, "she was going to Gungi's new home in Rampur, and then afterwards to her own home."

"Oh how I dislike her, too," said a dark brown one, dressed in a handsome gold-laced cloth, lifting her heavy bracelets up and pulling her rich gold cloth over her shoulders with a gesture of disdain. "She sets herself up for a rich woman when I know she has only two good *sarees* to her back; and it is shameful the way in which she treated that poor ignorant girl Kamala. The servant says that the girl had not even enough to eat, though of course she would never complain."

"The poor guileless one," said one of the widows, taking up the strain, "the other day when I questioned Kamala on the river bank she avoided me and said, 'Oh, they are all kind,' and when she gets a beating I can see it by the pained look in her eyes, and yet she would say it was all her fault, that she did not know her work."

"Not know her work?" said the woman near the

cushion, who was Bhagirathi's mother-in-law. "She works like a bullock, I have been told. I wish I had a daughter-in-law like that, instead of the firebrand that I possess."

"Why? Did you hear of Ganeshpunt?" said a married woman rather abruptly. "I hear that he is more and more to be seen in Sai's quarter."

"It is a shame," said an old lady who was distributing the betel leaves and flowers, and who was no other than Rukhma's mother-in-law. "I hear it is all their doing, getting the woman to come to their parties and even planning the meetings. People have eyes as well as ears. Poor Kamala! She is away now; and it is a good thing for her too. She will have to bend her neck and toil more and more hereafter in her father-in-law's house. I don't think her husband would care to take her away just now, seeing that the attraction is so strong elsewhere."

"No, the arrangement is that she is to stay with her father-in-law till the birth of her child. Of course it will be said that she is too young and inexperienced to go back with her husband just now, for, if she goes, she will have a time of it, I am sure, with Sai's attractions and the other girl they think of proposing for Ganeshpunt," said a widow with a sigh; and then added, "I pity her, poor girl; and she has not gone through the fifth month ceremony yet."

"This is the way they destroy our happiness," said Bhagirathi, bursting in; and when she saw the large company of women, ashamed at her boldness, she slid back to the door way.

"I knew she would come out like this," said her-mother-in-law grimly. "The girl has no manners and is getting worse and worse." Bhagirathi threw the twists of wet clothes down in the open quadrangle, and, making her vessel ring on the stone floor, left the room with a bounce. The jingle of her anklets was distinctly heard as she walked hastily out.

Rukhma's mother-in-law now rose to go. Just then Kamala's mother-in-law entered and was welcomed by all. Bhagirathi's mother-in-law took her by the hand and led her to a seat near herself. "The goddess Lakshmi has smiled in this direction, I see." "Which side has the sun risen to-day." "What good fortune brings you here?" Such were the remarks made on all sides. Then they began to ask the new-comer about Kamala. "She is with her father," said the old lady, curtly, "and we leave it to her husband to bring her or not as he likes. As for me I am fairly tired of that girl. She causes much disturbance when here. What with her mad fits of learning and her husband's foolishness, I really wish that she was not returning at all. Such a responsibility, too, and not at all like the other girls. She knows no work to be in any way useful, and when scolded she says that everything is her fault and that she will do better, instead of like the other girls taking it calmly or even sulkily. You know girls need scolding now and then, and sometimes one cannot help scolding them."

"Yes," said the fat woman, with a broad smile, "I know what you mean. As the old saying goes, 'The oil of the fried cakes is poured on the brinjals,' and the girl does not know this. Ha! Ha! Ha! So she is to stay at her father's till Ganeshpunt goes to fetch her?"

"And he will not be in a hurry to go, I suppose?" said Bhagirathi's mother-in-law.

"Did you hear about Bheema throwing herself into the well this morning?" said Kamala's mother-in-law, turning the conversation. "What a hubbub there was to be sure! I have just returned from the house. Rukhma has taken Bheema to her own home to shield her from the beating."

"What a foolish girl to do such a thing," exclaimed all in unison.

"The old woman, Bheema's mother-in-law, is very angry," continued Kamala's mother-in-law. "She wanted some of Bheema's jewels—the chain necklace I think—and coaxed her son to use his influence with his wife to get them. The weak-minded man—how foolish of him to listen to his mother, for the jewels were not really his. He used rough words, I am told, when Bheema refused to give them, and they had such a quarrel; and before her husband left the house Bheema went quietly to the backyard and threw herself into the well."

"Ah, how shocking!" said the old woman who was leaning on the pillow. "The mother of the man was stingy and cunning, and she must have pretended that there was no money in the house and induced her son to take from the girl the jewels. They say that the husband is very sorry, and they have hushed up the affair. But the girl had a narrow escape, and would have been drowned had it not been for our gardener."

Blame not the poor Indian woman for her love of jewellery. She strives and toils hard to put by a few rupees out of the money allotted to her by her husband for home expenses, and invests them in jewels. She knows well that they are the only things that will not be taken away from her at her husband's death or when any trouble or calamity overtakes the family. The jewels are hers whatever may happen to the other property. She sees her future independence in them, or at least has the consolation that she will have something to fall back upon in times of distress. It is a hard wrench when she is obliged to part with any one of them. Life is not so dear as these jewels are, for what is the use of living, she argues within herself, to be trampled on by others and to slave for others. Such feelings are purely Hindu, and are the outcome of wrongs committed for generations on the poor unprotected Hindu woman.

CHAPTER XIV.

"FATHER! My father! The night wind is cold, the moon is at its height. Do you see the waving shadows of the trees, the dark rocks there over the precipice, and the vast moonlit plain beyond? Oh, how silvery and shining everything looks!"

It was Kamala who was talking to her sick father as he reclined on the *pial* outside. He was better but still very weak. Kamala's mother-in-law had returned to Sivagunga, and the old dame was busy inside preparing gruel. Kamala was alone with her father. Her heart was full; it was so like the old days. The familiar murmur of the stream, the silent waving trees in front, and the rush and roar of the wind, all combined to recall the charm of those old days which were so precious to her. As she rested her head on her father's shoulder Kamala felt young again. "Oh, father! How much I have had to learn and how little I knew of the world when I left you! Why, father, why are you so different from the people in the city? You did not tell me half of what I ought to have known. I like the old life, I like it very much. Father! Father! keep me near you here always, and there will be no heart-achings over what people think and what they say. Oh! why should one's own people be against one? I am so afraid of offending and I do so offend everybody I come across. I don't think I have succeeded in pleasing anyone. There is my father-in-law, for instance. How I wish to love and please him, but I have done something wrong, and he does not care for me in the least. I fell at his feet before I came away, and said :—'Bless me Baba ! I am going home,' and expected that he would have said one kind word at least. But he was as hard as a stone, for after a time he calmly looked at me and turning his face aside said : 'Why do you fall at my feet ? Go ! wish me well to the *saniyasi*.' There was such a look on his face that I drew my *saree* over my head and felt as if I must cry. He must have been greatly disappointed with me, for I could see from the expression of pain and contempt in his face that I had done something to displease him. Oh, father ! he was not like this before. He was so different." Having said this, Kamala looked into her father's eyes and was silent. Her father's thoughts were evidently wandering, and he had not heard her. Just then a cloud covered the moon, and she felt a great hush in her soul as she also bowed her head in silent thought. It was some time before the silence was broken. Then Kamala spoke excitedly. "Oh, look there," she said, "the moon is peeping through the clouds and how wonderful and bright everything looks." "Do you know, father," she added after a little while, "that whenever I look over those silent moonlit plains, my thoughts wander far ? I seem to see scenes similar to these, but I cannot make out what they are. The pictures are dim and blurred. I seem to be journeying on and on and I feel some one near me soothing me with soft melodious words. It is not you, father, it must be some one else. Do you think it is mother; my mother? Oh, why do I not know anything of her? Tell me, father. The thought has crossed my mind that she may not have been what I should wish her to have been, and that is why you have been so silent about her to me. But now I cannot rest; tell me all, good or bad, she is my mother. Oh! how it hurts me to hear people speak about her."

The old man seemed unconscious of all this. He was seeing visions. Kamala recognised the old look in his eyes and was frightened. At last he spoke:— "Your mother! your mother! child. Ah, how shall I tell you about your mother? It breaks my heart strings to bring her back to my mind again. But I must tell you all, for I feel guilty in having kept her story from you so long. Shall I tell you how and where I first saw her? Can you imagine a fortress on a little hill. Think that the same silver moon yonder is shining on it, bathing its terraces and ramparts in glory and making the rounded temple tops in the centre shine like burnished gold. All round the fortress are huge spreading ancient trees, dark and solemn-looking in the soft pale light. Such a place was your mother's home, and I saw it for the first time on a night like this. High on the terrace wall in the deep midnight I saw some one walking. I thought it was the guardian deity of the sleeping fortress, for tall and stately, clear in the moonlight, appeared a woman's form on the terrace. The round full face seemed to catch the moonbeams as it was lifted up for a moment to the heavens, and then a rounded arm waved to some one below, and the figure disappeared.

This I saw from a distance, and when I hurried up to the village at the foot of the hill, I heard stories of a lovely grown-up girl immured in the fortress with her old decrepit father who had built a temple there himself and had surrounded himself with plundering devotees, and ignorant and superstitious priests. The old man had himself turned an ascetic after having given the affairs of his *jaghirdari** into the hands of his youngest brother and the bringing up of this girl to her aunt. This aunt I found out afterwards to be an aunt of mine too—my mother's step-sister, so here was a relationship, and I made up my mind to stay with her. None had seen the girl, for she had apartments and walks allotted to herself. I was not aware of the sacredness of the enclosures, and the next day when I went to see Droupadibai, my aunt, it was evening. As I got up the steps they directed me to the right, and there in front of me was a small temple. The air was still and heavy with the smell of flowers that grew thick around the temple. The trees were tender leaved as if newly budding, and they seemed to catch and retain in their golden crowns the rays of the setting sun. In front of the temple I saw a sight which made my heart throb with excitement. It was the sight of a lovely girl standing by the side of a gray old priest, who was bending over a tray of incense and ringing the soft bells ranged around it. The girl was startled, her heavy laced *saree* had fallen from her shoulders, and she looked like a wild deer frightened in its haunts. 'Is Droupadibai, my aunt, here?' I asked.

* A large estate.

"The girl lowered her gaze in an instant, and in modest silvery tones said: 'Droupadibai your aunt? She is mine too.'

"'And who are you?' I asked.

"'I am Dakli Bai' (the young lady), and then correcting herself, said, 'Lakshmi.'

"Frightened at her boldness in talking to a young man, she threw her cloth over her head and ran in. This was my first meeting with your mother. I cannot tell you, Kamala, what I felt. Droupadibai came out and the young girl came too. She had heard of her kind aunt's home at Sinhagud, and she lingered near to hear all the home news. The girl was unmarried, her ascetic father having thoughtlessly neglected to find her a husband. Droupadibai, good old soul, thought the matter out for us, and kept me with her as long as she could; and when I expressed a wish to marry her beautiful niece she gladly agreed to the proposal, and, quite against all rules, allowed me to talk to the girl. I found her one day sitting on the stone steps of the fortress wall, and there I spoke to her of my love, timidly at first. She blushed an innocent blush and withdrew, with her *saree* on her face. This she invariably did when I talked to her. She would not dare to lift her eyes to my face. But one day I was determined to make her talk. 'They want us to be married secretly. Will you be happy?' I said. She grasped the trunk of a tree for support and I boldly told her of my love. I told her that my home was far away, but that my love was great. 'Trust me. Trust me,' I said eagerly to her; and then she looked up, and said with such a look: 'I trust you.'

"Droupadibai insisted on the marriage ceremony being performed at once. All was done secretly, for they were afraid of the old father and thought of telling him afterwards and making it all right with him. But it proved to be a sad mistake. Droupadibai was in too great a hurry, and it caused us great misery afterwards. The very day after the marriage the old father came to see Droupadibai and told her that she was to prepare for the marriage of the girl. The girl was in great consternation, and Droupadibai and her husband did not know what to do. A very powerful neighbouring *jaghirdar* had asked for the girl. The only way out of the difficulty seemed to be for us to run away and then to tell the old man the whole story. It was thought that the marriage with a cousin would pacify him. Your mother thought otherwise, but her uncle and aunt insisted on her falling in with their own plan and she was brave.

"I remember distinctly the night when she came down through the temple corridors, over the echoing stone pavements, with her old uncle by her side. She looked more a princess, stately and firm, than one who was stealing away from her father's home, and her uncle was bending towards her with courtly deference, speaking to her of the arrangements made to convey her to her husband's home. When she descended the last step, leaving the fortress behind, I saw her stagger. For a moment her breath seemed taken away, for there, in front of her, lay a boundless plain, a wide expanse of earth and sky, with the silence, it seemed, of eternity resting on it. She had never seen this side of the fortress before. At her feet lay the great *tapa* tank, and a *pimpul* tree, huge, grey, and weather-beaten, stood near it. She held the tree and gazed for a moment as if lost in thought, and then with a sigh beckoned to her uncle to bring the palanquin. I was near her, but she gave me no look. Only when she was entering the palanquin she laid her small hand in mine trustfully, willingly, and I felt grateful to her. Then her uncle got on his horse and the aunt muttered her blessing on my wife and laid a casket of jewels in my hand, saying: 'Never part with this. It is an heirloom from Lakshmi's mother. Promise me solemnly.' Many a long dreary mile the uncle came with us, and he left us only on the borders of the Ghauts. My home was on the other side of the Ghauts near the seaside, where the waves beat round our rude walls.

"It took us some days to pass through the hills, and when I went home and proudly showed my bride, I found misfortune had preceded us, for my mother showed no joy at seeing us, and my sisters grumbled at the girl whom I had brought home. But your mother bravely bore their ill-natured taunts and jeers. It was only when they accused her of bringing misfortune with her that she cried and pined in secret, for, strange to tell, just about the time of our coming home, my father, who was once rich, fell into money difficulties. He had squandered his wealth in various ways, and when we went home we found him completely in the hands of scheming priests and astrologers, who got round the simple old man and helped him to spend what was remaining in feasts and charities to Brahmans and offerings to temples. The bare ancestral land alone was left to us. All this misfortune was ascribed to the coming of your mother, the white-footed girl, as they called her. They were jealous of the rich jewels she possessed but which I had promised her aunt solemnly that I would never part with. And I became tired of their open enmity, of their constant hankering after the jewels, till one day disgusted I left the home of my father's to go on a pilgrimage. Your mother, of course, accompanied me, and my sister's son, Ramchander, who was very fond of us also, came with us. He was learning the *Shastras* with me and I managed to instil into him, young as he was, some of the grand truths of our ancient books. We started for Kashi and visited many places on our way. Once your mother became very ill. This was when you were born. She called you Kamala, the lotus-eyed, because of your eyes. We spent two years in solitary places and were supremely happy.

"Oh, my Kamala! How can I give you a glimpse of those happy days? It falls not to the lot of many mortals to enjoy happiness such as we had. We lived in rude leafy huts, drank of the cool limpid streams; we rose with the birds, roamed through the echoing valleys and over far distant hills—hills where the soft white clouds lingered in the deep blue of the heavens. Your mother would walk by my side in the beautiful glow of morning and evening light, and as sunshine and shade played round her she looked like the goddess of the hills. We had our goats that came to us, our pet birds that came through the dark, tangled woods round our hut to receive their food from our very hands. A stream flowed past our hut and the giant *pallas* tree waved overhead. Your mother's only servant, who followed us all the way from her father's house, prepared our meals—boiled roots, sweet potatoes, rice, *dhal,* with home-made *ghee*, and simple cakes, and we were happy, supremely happy. Your mother read with me, with bewildered eyes, books that are never put into women's hands, and she was delighted when difficult portions were explained. Nothing came between her and me, and as her understanding unfolded, her love for me increased. It was a love too deep for words. Is it any wonder, then, that I love the mountains and the woods? They were kinder to us than human beings. But ah! our happiness was soon over. Before I realized how much your mother was to me, she was taken away from me. The look of pity and overflowing love in her eyes as she was passing away haunts me still. You know, my Kamala, you are very much like her. The resemblance struck me unexpectedly once, and that was at Dudhasthal last year. I was so overcome with emotion that I could not stop."

"Yes, father! yes!" said Kamala eagerly. "What about Dudhasthal?"

"What about it, child, what do you want to know?"

"Father! was I ever there before? It seemed so familiar. I heard your voice there and felt a strange feeling as if I have dropt into the cold rushing water and some one had rescued me. It was a woman's arm with bracelets on—I saw it drag me out. Everything was so plain, I thought I had seen it all once before. I rushed into the crowd as I thought I heard your voice."

"Did you, child?" And he drew her near himself and looked into her eyes as he used to do in days of old. "You have a strange memory. But don't you remember the face?"

"No, father, I saw only an arm."

"You had fallen into the deep pool, and it was your mother that pulled you out. You gave us a great fright then. It was on our way to the *Krishna Kshetra* and on the evening of that very day on the lonely road that your mother was attacked by the dreadful disease that carried her off. When she was very ill she said:—'Oh! what if you had lost your only child too? Don't be disheartened.' I remember it all. There was no one to help us. The owls hooted in the dark trees above us, the foxes cried in the dreary wastes around us, and the sound of other wild animals was heard in the distance. Your mother had a dream before she died. The yellow blazing palanquin that comes only for the saints came for her, and by it stood, she said, the *Yama* god, the dreadful *Yama*. She looked frightened and said that she was going. It was night, and the stars shone brightly and the winds moaned over the long, long wastes. The dogs that had gathered round us for the remains of our food barked as they rushed far over the hillocks. I knew she was no more. She had left me, but there was the happiness of the *swarga* depicted on her face. I looked at it and went through the last rites as one mad. After that I left the place with you, my only comfort."

CHAPTER XV.

WE will now return to Ramchander, whom we left conversing with Sai on his way to Sinhagud. At the next dark pass which they had to cross Sai left him saying that she would gȯ on in front to her village by a short cut, which she alone knew. Ramchander let her do so, and he leisurely followed by the usual route.

Sai's house was a low built one on the brow of a hill commanding a view of two valleys. The straggling village lay further on, and the *dharmashala*, or rest-house, was opposite Sai's house, with a deep hollow running between. Ramchander halted at the rest-house for some time, and went to look at the village. Sai, as soon as she entered her house, went by an underground passage to a room below, in which was seated an elderly man. In front of him were some brass images and flowers. His hand was on his beads, but his eyes wandered out through a low window that commanded a view of the village and valley in front. No one but Sai knew of the underground passage leading to this room, and the steep valley on this side of the house prevented people from even suspecting its existence.

"Dhaji bhavoo," said Sai, descending to the room excitedly, "I want you to tell me who exactly this new comer is. He seems to be a man from our parts. I heard accidentally of his relationship to the *saniyasi*

Narayen, from the great Bhagvandass, the *bhairagi* who was officiating in the house of Ramkrishnapunt, Kashi's father. Kashi is Kamala's friend, and Bhagvandass, the *bhairagi*, had introduced Ramchander to Kashi's family as skilful in medicine and as the *chella* (disciple) of Arunyadaya. The *bhairagi* accidentally mentioned to me Ramchander's relationship to Narayen the *saniyasi*." "I did not know him well and yet I feel as if I knew him," she said triumphantly. "He will pass this way as he returns from the village, and I want you to see him."

"Yes! It is always to get some information or other that you come to me now. You are the most fickle and the most wicked woman I have seen, and if you don't take care I shall expose you. You don't know what a sword is hanging over your head. They never forgive, the descendants of Raghopunt."

"I knew that," she said pettishly, biting her lips. "You need not so often remind me of that. It was you who took advantage of my girlish inexperience, you who ruined my life, and now you dare to say such things to me. I have to be as a cat near you. I have to attend to you, satisfy your foolish wants, and appease your foolish jealousies. I am tired of you. The less I see of you the better it will be for me and you." And Sai lifted her *saree* to her face. At this he gave her a sharp look and said, "Yes? Whine away, since that is all you are fit for."

"Stop your nonsense," she said snappishly. "Do you mean to say Sai cries before you. She cries before no man."

"Yes, when she has so many as her companions." Then changing his tone to a loud one of authority he said: "I have borne enough from you. Do you hear? I have given in too much to your pettish ways, and now if you stir from me even for a day I will expose you everywhere. I will tell who you are, how you ran away from your home and tried to pass yourself off as a woman of the vestal class, and that you are none such, but a Brahman. I will search for your husband and expose you to the revenge of the Raghavas. I will do all this and will have no mercy."

Sai heard him in silence. Then she said: "We shall see. But who is this man? First tell me that. Mind! I can defend myself against all your assaults. I will have my say too. No one can point to Sai and say that she behaved as one of the ordinary degraded class, that she took money, and sold herself, and so on."

"No! because you had enough money. But how did you acquire it?" he said, with a chuckle.

"How? Ask yourself, you dotard, and stop your nonsense. You are just as much to blame as I am if not more, and vengeance will fall on your head. You will see which is better, being put into prison or living independently the life of a prince with Sai."

The man put his head down at these words. He had a hang-dog look, and Sai cast at him a glance of withering contempt. Just then Ramchander was passing the road that curved through the valley in front. There was a man behind him and Ramchander himself was riding. Sai's companion in the room now rose excitedly, peered out through the window, and said in a whisper :—" I knew he was coming this way, he has passed this way before, and that is why I told you to be careful and stay with me. Did he see you?"

"Yes, I was with him half the way, and just left him and came by a short cut to be here before him. Do you know who he is?"

"Do you recognise the dress of the man behind him with the two-coned turban? He is the servant of the Raghavas, and he in front is your husband."

Sai held the wooden bars of the window for a moment, and then sat down, for she felt staggered. She watched the horseman pass and her feelings as she did so were hard to describe. "So this is Ramchander, my husband! How strange the name sounds in my ears now. This, the man who left me long ago in my mother's home, and ah! what a grand man too but I have lost him." For a time a great bitterness, passed over her soul. Her whole life came before her and the dreadful nature of the details connected with it. "How much I have sacrificed. Ah! what would I not give to have it even for a time?" She repented bitterly of her folly of running away. She was a woman who was moved by extreme emotions. Her knowledge of the world was great, and now that she had departed from the path of righteousness she relized the emptiness of the world and the people of the world. Her independence, once so attractive, now for a moment disgusted her. "What would I not do to change my lot :—to be virtuous and to be loved by one noble and really great? Ah! how I have been duped." She sighed and held on to the railings convulsively. All the while the man by her side was watching her face in an amused manner.

"The news has evidently given us food for much thought," he said.

At this Sai started as if from a dream, realizing vividly what was before her. "Ah!" she said, "it is all gone. You have blighted my life. You have made me what I am. I cannot be different, and yet I feel I might have been so different."

"Would you, though?" he said, with a fiendish grin. "Where could you have got your independence, your amusements, your daring pleasures, if I had not made you what you are?"

"Yes! you took away something from me—my name and my honour—I parted with them willingly, thinking of the glamour that you cast over learning, independence, riches, and the power of securing an influence over others. All these I possess. But what is all this without my name? However, there is no use crying over spilt milk. It is true Sai cannot be altered now. She cannot do without her independence. But come, let us forget all, and let us be friends once more."

Strange as this conversation may sound, it was indeed true that Sai had been betrothed to Ramchander during one of his visits home after leaving Narayen, the *saniyasi*. His mother, Narayen's sister, was anxious that her son should stay at home, and fearing that they might lose him as they had lost

Narayen, insisted on the betrothal ceremony taking place when Ramchander happened to be at home. But Ramchander could not stay long, as his heart was with Narayen and his master, Arunyadaya, to whom he had been introduced by his uncle. So, finding some pretext or other he left his home immediately after the betrothal and was not heard of for a long time. The company of Narayen and the studies he was engaged in with Arunyadaya had a peculiar attraction for the young man. The life of ease and pleasure he led at home disgusted him, and the betrothal was much against his will. Years passed, and when he next went home he found that rumours had reached his people that he had died, and that the girl to whom he was engaged, and whom he had only seen once, had suddenly disappeared in order to avoid the miseries of a widow's lot. But there was also a scandal connected with her disappearance, for the Brahman *pujari** of the house was found missing about the same time. On hearing all this Ramchander became more disgusted with his home and went back to Narayen. Just then Kamala was born, and Narayen's wife, who was very fond of the young man on account of his attachment to her husband, pacified him by saying that Kamala, her beloved child, would be one day given to him as his wife. Five years after Kamala's birth he was again called back to his home on account of his father's death, and he was obliged to stay there for some time to settle family affairs. In the meantime Kamala's mother died, and Narayen

* Priest.

in his great grief wandered far and wide with his little girl, and at last settled in Anjinighur, on the other side of the ghauts. It was thus that Ramchander lost sight of Narayen the *saniyasi*, whom he at last found again on the eve of Kamala's betrothal.

Kamala was more than a month at her father's house when Ganesh came to take her back. Somehow she did not now think of him as she did when she was at her father-in-law's house. The feeling that her happiness was in danger and that he might do something to ruin it had vanished. She had been in a disquieting atmosphere before. She had seen the wreck of the happiness of many young girls around her, and she trembled lest a similar fate should overtake herself. But now once again in the quiet security of her father's house and amid the old, peaceful, never-changing scenes her mind had become calm and placid. The cares and worries of the city life were left far behind. She was not even anxious for herself at this time. She seemed suddenly to have been lifted above the world. So when Ganesh came to see her, she met him calmly, almost indifferently, and when he expressed his wish that she should go to her mother-in-law, she acceded to his proposal and was willing to be taken away. She had had time to judge of his real character, for once the feverish anxiety about him passed away, she saw him with other eyes and became conscious of his weaknesses and failings. She had heard of the relationship in which Ramchander stood to her father, and she reflected with pleased satisfaction that that was perhaps the reason why she experienced a strange disturbing influence when in his presence and why those eyes of his had such power over her. It must have been the kindred tie, the blood relationship between her and him. Perhaps he was like her father and when later on she heard how he had nursed her father and cared for him she felt grateful to him. The incident at Dudhasthal, too, which had seemed so puzzling now became clear to her. Ramchander's kind thoughtfulness had prevented her foolish conduct from being criticized when her father was not near, and she was thankful to him. Once, but only once, a wish intruded itself in the deepest and most sacred chamber of her heart—a wish which made her blush at her boldness and cover her bosom with her hands as if to hide it from herself. Would, she said to herself, that Ganesh had been more like Ramchander. Such a wish, though natural it may seem, was shocking in the extreme to a Hindu girl, who must never allow herself to compare her husband with anybody else.

Kamala tried to feel joyful and happy in Ganesh's presence, but in vain. Her father was better and did not need her, but she could not understand his restlessness at times. "Has he not told me all his story; then why is he anxious?" thought the girl. Once or twice, before Ganesh came, the *saniyasi* took Kamala aside and said: "Kamala, if I were to die what would you do? Are you sure you are happy and that you do not need anything? You are not like your mother in this respect, and I cannot understand you. There must be true love between you and your husband and all will be well. You love your father too much, and I am afraid you are content to stay with me. I have not seen much of Ganeshpunt and I feel anxious."

"No, father, you are not to be troubled," said Kamala. "He is very kind to me, quite different from the husbands of the other girls, who often congratulate me on possessing such a good husband. I was once restless and anxious, but I don't know why, now I am not. He will be coming soon to see me."

It was a relief to the old man when Ganesh came, and he did not raise any objection to Kamala's going away at all. Ganesh had returned to his work at Rampur, but he came purposely to take her and leave her at Sivagunga with his mother. Kamala and her father took a long parting, and Ganesh felt very sorry for the poor girl, as he stood outside waiting for her. The mother-in-law met them at the foot of the hill; and Ganesh went his way to Rampur.

CHAPTER XVI.

AS Kamala and her mother-in-law neared their house, Bhagirathi was seen peeping over the wall in front of her own house. Kamala had a bundle at her waist, and her mother-in-law was far in front of her. Messages passed rapidly from Bhagirathi to the houses near, and before Kamala turned the corner of the street several heads peeped over walls and hedges and women clad in wet garments and with vessels full of water purposely stopped in front of their houses. "Welcome! Welcome! Kamala," were the first words uttered by Bhagirathi. "How are you?" "Where do you come from?" "Where are you going?"—were questions asked on all sides by ill-clad, shaven widows and by married women. Harni came running, but Rukhma, the usually happy Rukhma, looked strangely sad and thin. At her appearance, too, a sudden hush fell on the company. Kamala glanced at each inquiringly and at Rukhma in particular. Her sad, downcast eyes sent a thrill of fear through Kamala.

"What is it?" Kamala said, with questioning eyes, "what has happened? Tell me."

"Nothing, Nothing," said the elder women; as they abruptly turned to pass on to their homes. The smiles of welcome vanished and a dread fear seemed to fill their eyes as they whispered ominously to one another.

"He is better," said Rukhma with quivering lips. "We had the *vythia* (doctor) last night," and then, unable to restrain herself, she threw her head on Kamala's neck and wailed.

"Hush, child! you must not cry," said two or three near her. "You know she will get angry, the revengeful *Mari*.* Don't you know, no sound is uttered, no cry is heard, for those that she takes away? And it is bad to cry before anything happens. It is an ill omen."

Kamala was bewildered, and she turned for an explanation to Bhagirathi, who had now come out. "Hush! Hush!" said Bhagirathi, "Don't be frightened. It is not good to tell a new comer at once, but *Mari Aiye* has visited our town, and Rukhma's husband has been ill and two are laid up in our own house, the servant boy and the old cook, and we know not whose turn may come next. She cares for no one—she, the 'sacrifice demander' from *Yama* himself."

"Oh, how dreadful," said Kamala, trembling, and pressing Rukhma to herself.

Just then the front door of Kamala's house opened, and her mother-in-law was seen to look up and down the street. At the sight of the old dame the girls covered their heads more closely and dispersed, whispering, "We will see you again. There is so much to tell. Go now, Kamala, and be careful." The married women with their twisted bundles of washed clothes went to their houses, which they entered

* The cholera deity.

through the front door, whilst the widows entered by the backyard.

That night vague feelings passed over Kamala, and an awe and dread indescribable filled her mind. She had no sleep but lay morbidly wakeful, noting every sound and movement in the next house, which was Rukhma's. Her intense pity and sympathy for her friend made her feel as if she herself was passing through the same dread experiences. It was an agonising time, and in the stillness of night sounds fell on her ears with an ominous meaning. The moon paled and waned, the night wind rushed and roared, the owls hooted, their long mournful sounds seemingly prolonged over the dark rolling river, and the deep shadows of the trees at the back of her house appeared to her mind as if peopled by ghosts that night. And when the clouds hid the moon completely she paced her room uneasily. Then sounds of hurried steps in the next house attracted her attention. "Where was Rukhma? What was she doing? O God, what does this mean for my friend, the happy, bright, laughing Rukhma?" And Kamala cried bitter tears and wailed out, she knew not why:—"Spare her, spare her, this great misery." There had been the sound of restless steps and then there was a hush and a groan and next a loud cry—an agonising shriek that made her stand and shiver. It was the last rallying of the sinking powers, the last painful utterance of the departing spirit, which once heard is never forgotten. "Come near, near, near, I am alone," was shrieked out, and the wail quivered through the air, and then there was a hush. Then came smothered sobbings, and Kamala felt as if she were looking on the weeping Rukhma and longed to put her arms round her friend's neck and shield her from her sorrow. But ah! How could she comfort the breaking heart? And then came the last cry of the dying man before the soul made its entry into the other world; and Kamala fancied that she could hear the spirit crying even there! "Come near! Come near! I am alone. I am alone." The hush did not last long this time. There was a loud screech of the owls in the dark groves. A dog howled and then suddenly barked a short, sharp bark as if he saw somebody coming through the unseen air. Kamala threw her cloth round her head and hid her face. She knew what that meant. Dogs saw spirits. Dread *Yama's* servants were surely approaching. But what means this unaccountable silence in the house? O God, are they sleeping? Do they not know who are coming? Cannot the dread messengers of *Yama* be avoided? Can they not shut the doors against them? She felt she could see the dark shadows with the waving noose in their hands coming nearer and nearer towards the house. Was the sound of steps real? And then was heard a sharp bark, a great flutter in the trees yonder, followed by a great many barks and a rush of the dogs to the river banks. "Gone! Gone!" she said. "The soul is caught and taken away." Dark masses of cloud floated overhead and through them could be seen at times a weird pale moon. There were sudden shiverings and rustlings among the trees, with silences between. Then there was a stir in the house. A great wild wail that seemed to cleave the sky and then again a sudden hush, for the voice of a man in a strained unnatural tone was heard to say: "Cry not. Remove the body lest greater evils come." It was the voice of the young man's father and showed that his heart was breaking. Kamala covered her head and cried. The worst that she feared had come on Rukhma, and she longed for the dawn when she could fall on her friend's neck and cry, "Rukhma! Rukhma! What a lot is thine."

Kamala was not allowed to see her friend next day. The silence of superstitious fear seized all. Kamala imagined to herself what her friend had to bear; how her dearest relations would turn their faces from her and say: "Let her suffer, let her bear the sins of former generations, the unfortunate polluted one, who has been the cause of her husband's death. What sins she must have committed, how many hearts she must have broken!" And Rukhma, she knew how Rukhma would bear it all. How she would hide her face and mourn and not a soul would go near her to sympathise with her or say a kind word to her. Kamala became mad as it were with pain, thinking of all this. But the more she begged of her people to let her go the more they persisted in their refusal. And then came a time of trial and suffering which brought her firstborn infant into the world.

Kamala had to pass through days of great mental agony, and she often longed to be taken away to her husband's home. Her sister-in-law and her mother-in-law had become more bitter than ever, just when she needed their care and sympathy most; for now they openly told her in sharp cutting words that she was a burden to them and that her death would be welcome. "What a useless weight is left here," they would say. "She is fit for nothing—a drag not only on her husband but also on her people. How well Ganesh would have got on without her; but for the sake of the world one has to close one's mouth." And when Kamala's child was born they spoke of the infant as an additional load and burden on them. "Who needed a child just now, and that, too, a girl?" they said often. Poor Kamala hugged her new found treasure to her breast as if to shield it from all the harsh words and abuses that fell on its innocent head. Her superstitious mind trembled at the thought that their wicked words might blight the infant as curses were said to do. But when the bright eyes opened and the infant mouth smiled its unconscious angelic smile, she forgot all her troubles in the ecstasy of her new fond joy. "O God! Let me have this my treasure and I care not for anything they may say."

Two months passed and Ganesh came to Sivagunga. He was moved to see Kamala looking so wretched, but, strange to say, he looked on the child indifferently, and it smote Kamala to see that he found no pleasure in her babe. But all fathers are not expected to make much of their children, and she thought that it was the nature of men to be as he was. She was in ecstasies, too, at the prospect of going and living alone with her husband. Ah! what would she not do to make his life happy? She would watch his coming home and await his arrival with delicate morsels of cookery. The child would be brought out and she would gently endeavour to draw him closer to herself, and he would be sure to appreciate all that she did for him. Thus she gave rein to her imagination, happy in the thought that he would be perfectly happy and his delight would be in herself and her child. On the eighth day after its birth the child was named, and at the special request of Kamala was called Droupadi after her mother's aunt; for the story of her mother had taken a great hold on her mind and she had conceived a special fondness for the old lady, her mother's guardian, who was still living. There remained now only a single ceremony to be performed, and then Kamala was to go to her husband's home at Rampur.

Kamala had to pass through new and strange experiences in her city home. After a few weeks of quiet and peace the castle of happiness she had so fondly reared for herself was rudely dashed to the ground; and she soon learned how great injury a capricious and weak, though at times well meaning man, was capable of inflicting on a sensitive wife. Her husband's nature was cast in a rougher mould, and he could not understand the keen pain that his words and actions often gave to Kamala. He was kind at first, but Kamala soon found that his moods changed.

Kamala's sisters-in-law both lived in Rampur, and Ganesh often visited them. When he returned from their houses he always seemed quite a different man.

The venom that they poured into his ears made him silent and moody. This was at the commencement of their stay in the city, when Sai was absent from Rampur in her mountain home. One day after his visit to Ramabai, Ganesh told Kamala that his sisters had called her stingy and avaricious, and that they suspected that she saved without his knowledge and that was why he had not money to spare for them. This he told her frankly; and Kamala felt that he knew her better and that his confidence in her was not shaken; but sometimes when he came back and looked gloomy and would not open his mind to her she felt sad and desolate. Other little circumstances also happened that embittered her existence for the time being. He spoke thoughtlessly, and his words often cut deep into her heart and rankled there. They were just little incidents that led to such a strained relationship between husband and wife. One related to an upper cloth which was brought for sale by a merchant. Kamala thought that she had a right to speak out her mind about the article, which she considered very inferior, and when she was ordered to pay for it she went straight to Ganesh who was talking to Ramabai's steward, and told him that the cloth was not worth the money. Ganesh resented her interference, thinking that she regarded herself as superior to other women in having an independent judgment, and that she was too bold in speaking before a man who was intimate in his sister's house. He turned sharply on her and said: "Pay at once." The words were harmless, but the manner in which they were uttered frightened her, and she went in wondering what had come over him. But when after a time he came to her and said that she was a mean, low woman, no better than a grass-cutter, and that she needed shoe beating to bring her to her senses, she was shocked at finding how much her innocent interference had irritated him. Her response after a time followed timidly.

"There is no dishonour in bargaining, so why should I fear to tell the truth?"

"Yes! you don't care for anybody. Not even for your husband. Even I am as dust under your feet. I am nothing in your eyes."

"Why do you talk like that? Why do you listen to what your people say, and come and taunt me?"

The venom that her sisters-in-law had poured in his ears was at work and she knew it. Had they not called her over and over again proud, conceited, not caring for anybody, mean and stinting?

That was what made her refer to his people; but at those last words Ganesh was so exasperated that he said.—"My people! How dare you speak of them in that manner? I wish I could beat your meanness out of you. Everybody laughs at you, and even that man there was chuckling at your low grasping nature." She felt as if struck down by these words, and sat on the ground. She thought that something dreadful was going to happen, and almost cried her heart out.

Another little incident that occurred soon after made Kamala think that her husband had entirely lost his confidence in her and filled her heart with greater despair, for she felt disgraced and demeaned by it. It arose from her servant's carelessness; and she found to her sorrow that she as a woman was even less than a servant in her husband's eyes. It was but the old rooted prejudice in the Hindu mind against women; but to Kamala, brought up as she had been, it was all new, and her pain was great when she discovered that the mistake of a stupid servant was laid to hér charge. The servant was sleepy and did not take in an order given by Ganesh to buy three annas worth each of three different kinds of sweets. Kamala, to make things plain, had said: "Mind, quarter viss of each." Her husband had been more than nsually cheerful and kind that day. He was home from office early and said that he expected his sisters that evening. What, then, was Kamala's astonishment when the servant bought only a quarter viss of sweets in all. When questioned by Ganesh the servant looked stupid and defended himself, saying: "Ah! the *Bai Saheb* said quarter viss." Kamala turned to her husband with a smile and said: "How stupid! Did you not hear me say quarter viss of each?" But a look of disgust on her husband's face and a callous, sneering answer, "Who knows?" struck her dumb. Had he really lost all confidence in her? She sat down and murmured: "Yes! Who knows? Who knows?" till she felt almost mad.

Ganesh after a time seldom returned home early; and a strange restlessness came over Kamala, but she never disclosed to others what she felt. Even her faithful servant woman was a mere dumb looker on.

She dare not sympathise with Kamala, for the latter would not allow any one to pity her or say anything against her husband. But in a city it is impossible to keep one's conduct from being criticised by others; and Ganesh's conduct was being carefully watched by his neighbours. On one occasion a neighbouring woman visited Kamala; and with well-meant sympathy disclosed Ganesh's movements to her. After that came the silent acting of one of the most heart-rending dramas of life. Kamala used all her winning powers to coax her husband to come sooner from office, for she knew the cause of his staying away. He looked at her suspiciously at first, and then laughed and asked whether she had forgotten all the quarrels. Kamala put her head down and said that if her lord had forgotten she had forgotten too. She begged that he would never misunderstand her any more and told him how it cut her to the heart to think that he thought her mean and lying. Ganesh was good natured. So he promised to come soon the next day and did so. But ah! how disturbed he was, how absent. Kamala, suspecting the cause, wondered whether Sai was waiting for him in some of their well known haunts. "Was he thinking of Sai?" she said to herself. "Oh, that he should be false to me and attracted to her so!" He was positively miserable, she thought; he spoke not a word, but after gulping down some sweet cakes he rose and said that business called him out. What business, she thought she well knew, as she saw him going along the way leading to Sai's house. She went inside with a sigh and then for the first time after long months taking the mirror in her hand she looked at herself. She had changed terribly. Her miseries were telling on her. Her face had become thin. "Ah, Sai, Sai," she groaned, "why do you come across my path? Is not what I have to bear enough for me already?" The next day Ganesh looked crest-fallen in Kamala's presence; and at her direct words he put his head down like one guilty and made feeble efforts to please her. After he went out poor Kamala experienced another kind of feeling. She felt severe pangs of remorse at the thought that she had judged ill of her husband. Why did she argue with him, and utter such words to him? Perhaps he did not mean anything when he said: "Who are you to interfere with my pleasure?" The words had probably escaped his lips unwittingly; and she had taken them up and harped on them as only a mean woman would and made his life miserable. How very sad he looked in the morning; and now what would he feel? He would be more than ever estranged, he would feel that he was married to a woman who did not scruple to think everything evil of him, and he had been so noble, so good, so unlike other husbands, for he had really tried to please her often. She made herself miserable the whole day, crying and thinking of all her words, and putting her conduct in the worst possible light. No! she did not deserve to have a husband like him. How did she ever happen to say such cruel things? Oh, that somebody would trample her down and show her her own low mean nature, and then she would learn to avoid such mistakes. There were, however, grounds for Kamala's feeling miserable; and it was simply her own noble nature that made her accuse herself and bring herself low even to the dust at her husband's feet.

CHAPTER XVII.

AS days passed Sai even began to frequent the house and to come and go as an ordinary visitor. Whenever Kamala remonstrated with her husband or even alluded to Sai's coming so often, he silenced her by saying that there was no harm in the visits, and that it was a woman's low jealous nature that saw evil in everything. He even expressed surprise that she of all women was given to such jealous suspicions. The time, however, soon came when Sai visited regularly in the evening, and she it was whom he called immediately on his return from office, while Kamala sat out in the backyard long into the darkening night. Sai chatted and talked; and he answered in a gay spirit of raillery. Kamala he scarcely took any notice of. She thought of the time when if she was silent for a minute or absent looking in his presence, he made a great deal of her; and asked herself what had changed him so completely. His eyes now fell on her with a blight. His spirits were damped at the sight of her. "In what way is Sai my superior?" thought Kamala. She had a bold air of confidence and laughed and talked immoderately—Kamala thought, also immodestly—but she was not beautiful. She reminded her of a snake, especially when she looked askance at Kamala herself with an air of triumph. Kamala wondered how long this galling servitude and this miserable existence were to last.

One evening an incident happened which gave rather a serious turn to the situation. It was a festival day at Rampur. Ganesh had not gone to office; and so left home earlier than usual. Kamala had keenly watched him that day and had suffered intense mental agony at seeing him hurry out so as to avoid her company. She was standing at the door when to her surprise she saw Ramchander, her father's nephew, coming towards the house. He came dressed differently and not as usual in the mendicant's garb, and walked straight to the door of the house. Kamala, knowing the whole story of his life, did not wonder now at his appearance and the change in his dress. She felt suddenly as if she were living another life altogether. Her own mother's story came back to her mind, and she felt as if she were living in the higher atmosphere of her mother's house. Ramchander asked first for Ganesh, told Kamala of her father having been ill again in one of his mountain haunts, and of his own inability to come to the Rampur side. His own mother had died and he had to look after the affairs of his house and his property. He said that he might take Narayen with him or leave him near Arunyadaya as Narayen chose. He had to look after his own father's affairs as well, but messages would come for Kamala, he said, and she was to keep them informed of her welfare. He had come specially to inquire after her health at Narayen's request. He timidly hinted about the child. "Ah, a girl! Whom was it like?" and Kamala ran in to bring it and entreated Ramchander to stay till her husband came; but he said he could not as he had to go on to Anjinighur. He had just come from Sivagunga, where he had expected to see her. He had, however, seen her father-in-law there. To him he had told the whole story of her father's life, for her father thought that her husband's people should know all about her antecedents and that she would inherit all Narayen's property. Then he added a word of caution: "Be careful of Sai. I hear she is here." And when going he looked down a moment and said: "May you be happy, very happy, in your husband's love." At these words the tears rose in her eyes but she soon suppressed them. Ramchander looked at her kindly and said: "You know that after your father I am your guardian and you will have no lack! You must not cry. You are the happiest of girls, for if you want anything there is plenty at your father's house, and all will be at your disposal." With these words he hurried out.

Ramchander stood talking in front of the door inside the yard under the *neem* tree. All round were heads peeping from neighbouring houses. The servant woman, too, was listening to every word; and whispered to others:—"It is Kamala's relation for a wonder! Just fancy Kamala having a relation."

That evening Ganesh returned with Sai. Kamala did not appear disturbed, for her thoughts were wandering far away. She was anxious to tell her husband of Ramchander's visit, but Sai's presence, somehow, deterred her from doing so. Ganesh was, however, looking unusually disturbed and absent. Sai sat on the *zhopala* (a wooden swing) as usual, laughing and chatting, but this time with gleams of triumph which jarred on Kamala in spite of her outward calm. She jeered at the house, at the things in it, at the way in which they were kept, and not stopping there she even ordered Kamala, saying: "Here, get me that spittoon. Do some work at least, you evil faced girl!" Kamala appeared not to take any notice of her words; but something rose within her at the sight of Ganesh's unaccountably troubled and depressed look. She thought that the sooner the whole farce was ended the better. What cared she even if she lost her life? The pride that made her calm and indifferent suddenly left her, and the independent spirit of her parents, the spirit that made them leave their homes, preferring hardships to a life of luxury, was not altogether absent even in the gentle affectionate Kamala. "Don't you hear, you deaf lout?" said Sai, and turning to Ganesh, "Look at her: she does not mind me at all. Make her do it." Kamala was sitting with her back turned and her head on her knees. She was astonished at the turn of affairs. Never before had Sai behaved like this. Her husband's voice fell on her ears. "Here, rise and do as she tells you." With these words she felt a severe thump on her back and she rolled a few steps. But the tiger element in her nature was roused. She got up, suppressed the pain, and facing him said :—"You! You! to strike me for this. Take care that God does not strike you in return." He felt awed. It was an unusual thing for a woman to behave in this fashion, but she faced him and stood her ground. And emboldened by her victory she cried to Sai :—"Leave my house for ever. Leave at once. If you do not go I shall force you." And with extraordinary strength she pushed her out, while Sai kept appealing to Ganesh. But Ganesh seemed rooted to the ground as it were, and Kamala shut the door on Sai and returned, and saw that her husband stood where he was. After that she felt lifeless. The excitement of the moment had passed, and she sat down on the floor and gave vent to her feelings. Sobs, deep sobs, seemed to choke her. Her husband at last broke out :—"What have you done, you *Avadasa*. You have disgraced me before the public now. What shall I do? How shall I show my face outside? Are you not satisfied with the disgrace that you have already heaped on me that you add this too?"

"What have I done? I have done nothing," said Kamala. "I have only sent the woman away who took my place and who had not even the prudence of a dancing-girl, but who was brazen-faced enough to order me to work for her—me your lawful wife whom you loved so dearly once." Then she added passionately: "Why do you, my husband, do all this? Why can't we be happy as before for our beloved child's sake at least?" And she threw herself on the ground and clasped his knees.

"Yes! why?" said Ganesh with a cold contemptuous look at her; and then turning away from her said :—"You to talk to me like this in the face of what you have done, you, who are worse than Sai herself. You have already disgraced me and you shall suffer for it."

"Disgraced you? Why! what have I done?"

"Why do you feign ignorance, when I can read you through and through, when I have seen with my own eyes the man loitering about here?"

"What man? Of whom are you talking? O God! what is this?"

"You may well feign astonishment, but you cannot deceive me. Our forefathers' saying is true—'Never trust a woman.' You pretended to care for me in order to cast dust in my eyes, to make me believe in you, and leave you by yourself." And grinding his teeth and stamping his feet, he said: "You shall suffer for it. Why do you fall at my feet? You can put on the appearance of innocence very well. Just now you nearly staggered me and I thought you were innocent, I felt for a moment the old feeling, but it is gone. I see you in your true colours. I shall swear the child is not mine and turn you out."

"What, so much, would you really say that it is not your child? Ah, welcome death! I don't even want to know the name of the man you suspect. You to think of me like this. Who has told you this tale, for if you really think like this I shan't live long to trouble you? Do think again before you accuse me."

"What is there to think? I know what is true," said Ganesh coldly and sneeringly.

"Oh God! Why do you talk like this?" An icy chill passed through her at his strange sneering manner. She felt something bound round her heart and choking her. Suddenly she seemed to grow ten years older in experience; and standing up she said in a calm voice: "Kill myself I cannot; that would bring you into trouble. God will reveal the truth; but I will not stay here any more." Then she told him that if anybody asked about her he was to say she had gone to see her father who was ill. "It will silence all evil tongues and no disgrace will be attached to you."

"Here is some money," he said, looking pitifully at her. "No, I don't want any money. You shall never see me again." Something made her shudder and tremble as she walked, and she clasped her child and rushed out on to the dark silent road. Before she went out, however, she checked herself and called the servant woman to follow her, while Ganesh quietly looked on. She had not gone many paces before she stopped under a tree. The winds were howling on all sides and the darkened tree-tops rustled ominously. A long desolate plain lay before her. She said to herself: "Where shall I go? Not back to my child home at Anjinighur. No! Never! Never! A woman must die in her husband's house, and never return to her own home." Then a thought seized her and she almost ran on while the servant woman followed behind remonstrating. "Don't tell any one where I am going," she said. It was the most unlikely place that she made up her mind to go to. It was back to Sivagunga to her father-in-law's house. "It is they that must have put the idea into his heart; and I must go to them and live my life out with them."

The darkness thickened as she passed along a weird road that lay between two paddy-fields. The passion in her soul was driving her on. In vain the servant woman called to her and she madly clasped the infant to her breast, and scarcely stopped to hear the words. Her heart beat wildly and her head throbbed. At last through sheer exhaustion she sat down. "So this is what has come of all my strivings." The words, "This is not my child," rang in her ears with a terrible wildness, and she said: "Ah! what shall I do? Where shall I hide myself. How shall I destroy myself? Oh! welcome death, but how difficult it is for *Yama* to come. I implore thee, *Yama,* come." But what if death would not come. The future—the dreadful future—seemed to thrust itself before her. Death was her only solace; and she lifted her head up in wild agony. But what was the strange feeling that overcame her now? She felt suddenly a new experience that she could not describe. Above her head lay the vast expanse of the heavens with all its myriad glittering stars; and its silent immensity seemed to strike a thrill through her. The thought darted across her mind—What am I in this great universe, and what matter if I live or die? Just then her little girl woke, and seeing her mother gazing at the heavens, pointed her infant hands to the sky, and gave vent to a wild *whoo* of delight. Kamala was struck by the gesture, as little things will sometimes strike us. It harmonised, she thought, so well with the great silent magnificence of the scene above and she thought within herself: Was the child appealing to God? Who made this unconscious innocent infant life, and who would take care of it after she died? Living things were cared for in some way or other; and a God—a wise, loving God—must be over all. She felt greatly calmed, and bowing her head ceased to think of the past. In the calm that came over her soul a message seemed to be whispered into the inmost recesses of her heart: "No, you must not die. You must live and show what a life of true innocence can be. You must win by love, win all hearts—stoop low, for nothing is mean. Arise and work, for your work lies in this world." She rose refreshed. A new life seemed to spring within her. The selfish sorrow vanished. She was going to live for others now and even for those who hated her. She would love, and show what love and innocence could do. She would bear all, even if they trampled on her; and one day Ganesh would know of it too. A soft sweet glamour spread over her and she was happy in the great sacrifice of self she had contemplated. It may seem strange that an experience such as this should have been felt by an ignorant Hindu girl. But even a savage is known to be impressed by grand inspiring scenes of nature, and Kamala, moreover, was different from other Hindu girls, in that she had a highly cultured father and a learned mother; and she had herself learnt to feel and think.

CHAPTER XVIII.

SEVERAL circumstances and influences combined produced the change in Ganesh's conduct which led to his acting towards Kamala in the manner he did. He had hitherto steered clear of any troubles and had tried not to offend Kamala, but all the time he was getting more and more involved in Sai's clutches. Sai and he met behind the temple groves accidentally, it would appear, on several occasions. She began an intimacy with him only with the view of taking revenge on Kamala. Ramchander's callousness towards her had incensed her terribly, and she was determined to make the girl whom he thought so much of suffer in some way or other. Ramchander had wished Kamala to be happy in her home and he had said that he would be happy in her happiness. It was a new representation of a pure love to her, and she was angry with herself and envious of Kamala. She loved to have people at her feet, and she felt that Ramchander almost spurned her though he was intensely polite and obliging. Sai had contrived to meet him on several occasions in the mountain haunts, and in all their meetings he had maintained a quiet dignity and a proud reserve. Sai did not care for Ganesh much at first, because she considered him young and spiritless. But she exerted herself to make him her slave so as to induce him to neglect Kamala and even to send her away. She was also aware of the low esteem in which she was held by Kamala, and that was another cause of her hatred. She had a subtle attraction for Ganesh. She talked and laughed and exhibited a freedom and independence which seemed to him most fascinating. The more he was in her company the more she exerted herself to please him, till at last she found herself watching for him in the evenings and getting restless when he did not soon appear. Quick and sharp as she was she did not somehow grasp the other side of his character, his wish to please all and avoid troubles, and when he stayed longer than usual with her, a pleased soft expression would steal into her eyes, those eyes that were usually sparkling and keen, and the lips would part in a shy, pleased smile. It was a bewitching look. Ganesh caught the infection of her bright spirits, and he too got into the way of talking in a bright off-hand manner, and excelled even Sai in her keen witty sayings and clever repartees. Sai was astonished, and she who wanted merely to play with the man found that her affections began to be set on him. She tried to keep him long by her side and appoint places where they would meet as it were by accident. It was thus that they met behind the temple grove on the day on which Ramchander visited Kamala at her house.

"Ah! how late you are to-day," said Sai, when Ganesh came.

"Am I?"

"Yes! you ought to know that. See what a sight you have missed. That temple top was blazing with silver and gold as the sun touched it through the cleft of yonder hill; and the tank there in front,—the large sacred tank, whose bottom no one has fathomed, and in whose bosom, they say, a whole city lies engulfed—was as calm as a crystal and mirrored a moment ago a gorgeous city. From whence came those domes that I saw distinctly, those large mansions, and those broad paved streets? It was a silent city, a city of the dead, and I thought the enchanted moment had come, when, the sages say, a convulsion will take place and when the whole buried city will rise out of the lake, silent, solemn, and entire, the waters being swallowed up in the womb of the earth. Do you think such things are possible? Can you explain them by your wonderful new knowledge acquired in schools. When you did not come . . . Well! . . . There you missed a treat, and that is all I can say. Come! If you like we shall sit on the edge of the lake."

"Yes! we have nothing else to do. I was thinking of Kamala, how she would have enjoyed the sight." These words just escaped his lips unawares. Perhaps he had felt a twitch of remorse at the sight of Kamala's face as he came away, but he soon checked himself. Sai looked at him hard, and tossing her head said:—"*She* does not care. Do you think all have the soul to enjoy such things? She is accustomed to staying at home."

"Yes! when we make them stay, the poor souls."

"Do you mean to say she cares much for you and the places you visit, and natural scenes such as these? I know where her thoughts are just now," said Sai looking much incensed.

"Her thoughts! where can they be?"

"Not with you, surely."

"Then with whom?" asked Ganesh, with a smile, complacently looking at her.

"Don't you know the grand cousin she has, who adores the very ground she touches? What are you compared with him? Clever and learned and rich enough to buy you up even."

"I don't know of any such person. The *saniyasi* her father is poor enough and she knows none."

"Your heart is with her and that is why you excuse her," said Sai with flashing eyes.

"Why? what do you know? I like to see you angry, for you look so pretty, but why are you against my wife?" Ganesh was bent on mischief partly, and he wanted to arouse Sai's jealousy.

"I am not against her. I only show you where you are loved truly and where you are deceived. Kamala seems no doubt innocent and guileless."

"You must not talk of her like that. There are bounds to everything, and talk about a wife is always distasteful to her husband."

"The poor dove! That is why you leave her so much to herself."

"It is for you I leave her."

"Why do you do so?"

"I don't know," and he tried to hold her hand.

"And you, you think that such as I am am not worthy to talk of your wife?"

"I did not say that. Don't be angry."

"I who reserve all my time for you, I who try to

please you. What does your wife do? She does not give two thoughts to you. I tell you that even now perhaps she is talking to her lover. I heard of his coming before I came here, and even saw him inquiring for your house."

"How dare you say such things? She knows nothing of anyone's existence, and she talks to no one in her husband's absence. Don't try to make me angry." This he said seriously.

"Come, let us see," she said.

"See what? Are you playing with me?"

"I tell you she knows him, and I can tell you a great deal more, too."

"You cannot, you dare not. Let us go and see."

"Not so fast, not so fast. We shall go to Sarangapani's *wadi*, which is empty, and from the window overlooking your house we shall see if Kamala is talking or not."

As they went she pointed laughing to a gaily trapped horse that was standing at the corner of the street. But Ganesh was furious. He thought she was acting a great lie to torment him; but lo! from the window, what did he see? The woman laughed and hissed in his ears 'fool,' and he held the window and strained his eyes, breathing through his compressed teeth. Was it Kamala, his own wife, standing near the half-opened door so suspiciously, and a man in front under the *neem* tree, half-hidden from the road? Kamala, the penniless, when did she come to know of this stranger's existence? He turned with questioning eyes, and Sai divining his thoughts turned away her head. She felt a throb of pain at his great suffering, and a momentary inclination to explain all came to her. But when he turned fiercely on her and said with a hoarse voice: "Are you satisfied?" the fiend in her nature was aroused and she retorted angrily: "Satisfied? why should I be satisfied? fool that you should feel so much for her. Why! she is an old hand at it all. I got it from his very lips that he saw her at Dudhasthal, too, I am sure without your knowledge, for you don't seem to know anything about him. Did I not say, Be careful of a *saniyasi's* daughter? He is the distinguished *chella** of Arunyadaya and Narayen's nephew and attendant, even the very man that summoned Kamala to Anjinighur when her father was ill. Now do you understand? Do you recognize in him the clever physician who attended Kamala? For after he came was not the cure miraculous?"

Ganesh groaned. "Stop! Stop!" he said. "But it is all true. Go on." But after a time—it seemed an age to him—he said: "Come, I will have my revenge. You shall live with me and I shall get the truth out of her, but she will be made to feel the tortures of hell. Come, let us go home."

"Not so soon. You must take some food. You must not make a hubbub. Act the part of an unconscious husband and everything will be out. I don't like to see a quarrel. You can quietly send her away. I shall come and stay an hour or two to-day."

What happened afterwards has already been told. Now the reader will understand Ganesh's behaviour.

* Disciple.

Kamala reached her father-in-law's house in the dark hours of the early morning. Nerved with a new strength she had passed along silent, deserted roads, undaunted either by the great gloom in the mango topes or by the thought of the ghastly tales she had heard of robberies and murders committed on the way by which she went. The servant woman in terror begged her to stop at the rest house for the night, but Kamala was determined to go on; and the two women glided like ghostly shadows through the darkness, unnoticed by any one. Once they heard some steps behind, but they were themselves objects of terror to others; for such is the power of Hindu superstition that a woman seen in a dark night in unfrequented parts in India is sure to be taken for a walking-demon, from whose clutches there is no hope of escape. As Kamala reached her father-in-law's house she felt a momentary sinking in her heart. How cruel and heartless did they all seem formerly, and how would they look upon her now? "No, I must not be daunted, my life-work is here," she said, breathing quickly, and knocked firmly at the door. It was an unusual thing to hear a knock at this early hour. Ganesh's father himself rose to answer it, and came out with a flickering oil light in his hand. Kamala on seeing him, bowed herself to the ground and groaned: "Take me in, I have come from far."

"Why? What?" stammered the bewildered old man. But seeing the servant woman just behind with the child he changed his tone and ordered her to go in. Then in a commanding tone he asked Kamala to rise and come in and explain matters. "I enter your house only on one condition, that you tell no one that I am here, that you will protect and keep me, however unworthy I may seem. I will slave for you —will do anything. Only this boon I ask. I want to be unknown. I do not know what to tell you. I am an outcast now, and only fit for death; for my husband has turned me out, or rather I have left him. He suspects me. Oh! how shall I tell you? How can I utter the words he spoke even before you?"

"What is it all? Why all this ado?"

"Ah! he has said you know not what. But is it not you people that have put him up to it? I have come to prove my innocence."

"But what is it?"

"There was no turning him. He ground his teeth and hissed into my ears more than once that I was false to him. Why did you put him up to it? Drive me, kill me, but ah, this falsehood I cannot bear. Did I give any one reason to think such things?"

"Hush! you are talking madly. Arise, you are not in your senses. Perhaps the bad news about your father has been too much for you. No one put any such dreadful idea into your husband's head. Come, your mother-in-law must tend you. Don't sorrow, my child. After your father am I not also one?" At these words Kamala simply stared. Why were they so unaccountably gentle and loving? Her father was not dead, he was only ill, and yet her father-in-law was so kind. Ah! how harshly she had judged him before. She had expected a scolding from him and words such as these :—"If your husband suspects you there must be ground for it, and we cannot have you here." But what was all this? She stood rooted to the ground, and her father-in-law felt confirmed in his opinion that she had lost her senses. After a time she turned to the old man, and, with the faint glimmer of a smile on her face, said, "So you do not think anything evil of me."

"No, we don't, child. How strangely you behave!"

"It may seem strange, but I am not mad," said Kamala calmly. "I saw Ramchander-punt yesterday, and he told me all the news of my father's illness. But somebody has caused your son to believe that I am wicked, and now it makes me fear that he is more mad than I am. That woman Sai comes in the evening, and he has of late been so depressed and so different that I cannot but think that it must be her doing. She has given him the fatal drug. I must stay with you. You attend to him, but do not tell him where I am."

Both husband and wife listened with great concern; and then they took her inside. The mother-in-law in her room broke into lamentations, whilst Kamala comforted her. Kamalā suspected not the great sorrow that was in store for her. Only that night, a few hours before she came, they had heard of her father's death from a messenger who had come in search of Ramchander, and the old man kept the news from the distracted girl. They treated her with love and tenderness, but Kamala knew not that the change in their treatment of her was brought about chiefly by

Ramchander's visit. She was not the penniless girl they imagined her to be, but a rich heiress far above them in birth and position; and all her previous faults were now ascribed to ignorance and innocence. The mother-in-law, in her usual excitable way, drew flattering pictures of Kamala, and the old man, who had always had a strange partiality for her, smiled at the good turn affairs had taken. He said:—"Did I not tell you from the commencement that she was above the ordinary run of girls?" Before Kamala came they had determined to call her home and treat her with all due consideration.

"Ah! there is compensation even in this world," said the happy, trembling Kamala. "I get all this attention when I thought that the whole world was against me."

CHAPTER XIX.

IT was a quiet peaceful evening. The long dewy pasture-lands lay bathed in a yellow light and the last smile of the sun flickered on the grass that covered the slopes and the distant meadows, so soft and pliable that even the gentlest breath of wind made dimples in it. The old, old peaks were there, and a heavenly radiance seemed to rest on their tops and on the wide plain beyond, revealing every object that came into view. The dark rocks, enveloped in the yellow shimmering light, seemed to be instinct with life; the huge spreading trees far away on the plains were spangled with gold; and the dead leaves quivered as if they too were alive. It was such a scene that met Narayen the *saniyasi*, as he lay in his grass-thatched hut on the ledge-like plateau in his old mountain retreat where Ramchander found him after Kamala's marriage. The rush of the torrent was heard distinctly close by, but the *saniyasi's* thoughts were far away, and his mind was grappling with a new and distinct problem of life. The nearness of death seemed to have deprived him of all consolation in his usual philosophical thoughts. The highly sensitive soul was about to shake off its mortal coil and face—what? Was there really a soul?. What became of man after death? A few months before he could have answered these questions with self-satisfaction, but now, as the gates of death opened, a dread fear overwhelmed him.

Had he after all been deceived? *Nirvana*—the absorption of the individual into the Deity—this was the spiritual goal he had all along been aspiring to, but what if the end should prove to be the complete loss of consciousness and the annihilation of thought? In that case what would become of all his abstract meditations, all his fastings and prayers, his suppression of passions and all promptings of self? In what way was one like Arunayadaya superior to the unthinking crowd? But even Arunayadaya, who possessed the vision of the seer and the faculty, under great mental excitement, of knowing what was happening to those he loved, even he had not explained to him the mystery of death. He had been rewarded no doubt to a certain extent for all his meditations and abstractions, for he had attained a solemn placid happiness, a calm unknown to many. The world had been nothing to him. Riches, name, position had all lost their power over him. Sorrow had been overcome and cares had been left behind. But even Arunayadaya had often talked doubtingly of the hereafter. Surely thought did not become extinct for ever? Death must after all be a long sleep during which thought is only suspended. And then what was to be the nature of the future state? Narayen shuddered at the bare thought of annihilation. He was evidently groping for more light, for a more definite revelation of the spiritual and the supernatural, but his was a noble soul, and notwithstanding his imperfect knowledge he had tried to lead a noble life. After a time he felt calm and soothed. It appeared as if the earth had been taken away from under his feet. All ties and trammels had fallen off completely. The light of the sun had by this time assumed a pearly haze and the stars were beginning to peep out. The breeze came gently sighing and seemed to become part of the whole tranquil scene. The soul of the *saniyasi* drank in for a moment the peace and tranquillity of nature all around. Is it in this way that we cease to live to the outside world and live only with the stars and the gentle breezes? But this sweet calm lasted only for a short while. There fell a sudden gloom in the hut, and Narayen felt he was striving for something definite, something that he could be sure of. "Oh! for faith to strengthen me at this hour," he cried aloud, and then fell into a swoon. After a brief interval, he breathed his last troubled breath and was no more. Arunayadaya came too late to be recognised by his disciple, but according to his own request the body of the *saniyasi* was taken and buried in the silent forest of Panabras.

The news of the *saniyasi's* death was gently broken to poor Kamala by her father-in-law; and she mourned many a day and night for the beloved Dada whom she would see no more. But harder trials awaited her. After a time, when she was just beginning to be reconciled to her lot, her little child took ill. Those bright eyes that cheered her once had an ominous far off gaze, and though the lips always parted with a smile and readily gave a soft, ringing, bounding laugh, the child seemed very different from other children. When Kamala felt distressed, the little eyes looked into her face with such a sympathetic gleam that the poor mother felt afraid and clasped her little treasure to her bosom as if to hold it there for ever. As days passed the child became thinner; and a low fever consumed its highly sensitive little frame. Then Kamala's superstitious fears were aroused. To the Hindu mind the spirit world is a world of reality; the universe is inhabited by living spirits, good or bad, of departed human beings; and these spirits are supposed to possess qualities which were theirs during their human existence together with other qualities peculiar to spirits. The ordinary belief is that spirits before entering *swarga** have to pass through a preliminary existence in this world, the period of such existence varying according to the life led in this world during the human existence. If the being leads a good life by doing deeds of charity, and has acquired a mastery over self, then he passes straight to *swarga*. But if he has not so lived his spirit has to pass through a long period of probation, and some never even attain to *swarga*. It is these spirits that are dreaded most. Children are said to be specially susceptible to the influence of such. The credulous mother often sees this widow demon in her dream, who generally appears with another child in her arms and asks the mother to accept it. Against this evil power, however, it is supposed that the temple gods and the household deities possess a protecting influence. The distracted mother often has recourse to exorcism to free her infant from such fatal influences

* Heaven.

Even Kamala was not free from such fears, and the servant woman who always interpreted her dreams for her filled her head with all sorts of superstitious notions. Kamala did all that she could for her infant, but the child was no better. At last she heard that a great god was about to manifest his presence in the plain opposite the Bhavani temple, and she determined to take her child there. As she approached the temple she saw a large procession moving towards it from the opposite side. People were rushing about distractedly and yelling at the top of their voices. The procession stopped some distance away and then a circle of frantic devotees was formed which became larger and larger. Kamala stood under a tree trembling and silent, watching the procession, with one arm outstretched to the god and another clasping the child to her bosom. She had braved much in thus coming here. The dear little weakling lay pining in her arms but the full beauty of its lovely eyes was turned towards its mother. Nearer and nearer approached the procession, and narrower grew the circle round the dancing devotee. Then a sudden fear seized upon Kamala. What if the blind deity were to strike her little one dead before listening to her petition? The gods always wanted an offering; what if they demanded the best and the choicest—her own little treasure? Ah! she would have flown away with it to the ends of the world to protect it. The child had heard the shout; and its eyes were fixed on the procession. Then they turned towards the mother with an enquiring gaze—

such wondering round eyes they were. Kamala knew the look well, and she hugged her child to her bosom and cried out:—"O God have mercy. Not this darling one. Don't ask this. Take me away, but spare her." The child's cherub face nestled to her bosom, and the soft eyes, once more taking a look at the mother, closed. She felt the head, it was warm and throbbing. A sharp pang passed through her heart. "It is not better after all." Had she done wrong in coming? No, she would make one more appeal. Was the fever increasing? She fell on her knees and prayed a silent prayer. People thought she was mad. The procession went by. After a long time she got up. Her child was sleeping, and shivering all over. She made haste to return home.

* * * *

The night was dark, and there was only a faint glimmer of star-light in the low room in which Kamala was seated with her child. Outside, however, the stars shone brightly, and the wind moaned and sighed with a sad, sad wail. "Sleep, my child, sleep!" said Kamala, as she looked with agony at the pale wasted face on her lap. The eyes once more opened wide, and she hugged her child to her breast and said: "Don't look like that—sleep, dear one, sleep," and then in a low voice she murmured a plaintive melody, the words of which seemed a mockery, for the infant had not long to live.

"Golden is thy cradle,
Wide thy father's sway,
Gently slumber, sweet one,

Harm is far away.
Sleep, little one, sleep.

Bending o'er thy cradle,
All to thee unknown,
Kindly spirits hover,
Seen by Heaven alone.
Sleep, little one, sleep.

Guardians of thy slumber,
Of no earthly race,
With their wings they shade thee,
Gently fan thy face.
Sleep, little one, sleep.

Light upon thine eyelids,
Falls their kiss divine,
Lip to lip they mingle
Spirit, sweet, with thine.
Sleep, little one, sleep.

Never yet so lovely,
Luscious on the bough,
Cluster of wild berry,
As my babe, art thou.
Sleep, little one, sleep."

As she sang this familiar song each word sounded strange in her ears. Tears flowed fast from her eyes. It was more a death song than a lullaby, and she pressed her child closer and closer to her breast. Did she know that time was speeding, and that the star-light now shone on her child and herself? And did she know that the infant spirit had taken to itself wings when she was singing the tear-woven melody? Kamala sat cold as a stone with the child clasped to her breast, and the morning found her in a dead faint leaning back on the wall. They thought the mother and child had both gone; but the one revived to the consciousness of an aching void that would never be filled, and the other had flown away.

When Kamala awoke she had a raging fever that made her unconscious for days afterwards. She knew not that another great wave of trial was passing over her. To the neighbouring people she seemed to be the buffet of fate, and they said that the star of baneful influence had shone at the hour of her birth. What were all her riches to her now? She had lost the greatest adornment of a woman. Ganesh had suddenly died of cholera after twelve hours' suffering. Great consternation filled the house, and Kamala herself was found at the point of death. Her father-in-law and mother-in-law had to proceed to Rampur, and her friends nursed her in turns. Days passed, and she awoke from her unconscious state, but only to misery such as seldom falls to the lot of woman. Without father and mother, degraded and despised, a creature of ill-omen, she hid herself from all around and cried in the secret of her heart for her lost treasure—her little babe. She looked upon her husband's death as a meet punishment for having left his house, for was it not different now with her friend Bhagirathi, the scornful fiery girl? Her busband had left his mistresses and come back to her, and now she was happy, boisterously happy, in the possession of a firstborn son. Bhagirathi had told Kamala that it was through her own fault that her husband had been estranged from her; that she had been jealous and spiteful and had taken every opportunity to upbraid and defy him, and that after the birth of her son she had found out her mistake. Bhagirathi's husband had told her that he had never cared for anyone else, and that it was only to punish her that he had behaved as he had done; and Kamala felt a keen pang of remorse when she thought that if she had stayed with her husband it would have been all right with her too. But now the widow's blight had fallen on her. She who wanted to win others by her good deeds and justify her innocence in the sight of her husband's people, was now the most accursed of all, and she felt she deserved all this misery. Her old friends and acquaintances, however, gathered round her, and did all they could to alleviate her sorrows. Kashi brought her infant child and laid it in Kamala's arms, saying :—"It is not my child. Nurse and bring it up." And Kamala found some crumbs of joy still left in this life for her.

CHAPTER XX.

A couple of years passed; and then Kamala came to know something which, though painful from one point of view, served to soften her rugged life and cast a glimmer of light on her path. It was the light of a love that was so unselfish, so strangely strong, and so utterly beyond her, that she felt almost lifted, as it were, to another world. It is true she felt that that love could never be hers, and yet in a way it was hers for ever, and she was satisfied. The secret was revealed by Ramchander one evening in her favourite spot overlooking the river at the back of her house. She was sitting and meditating as of old on all the past incidents of her life when she saw Ramchander approaching. She had not seen him for two years, and her heart bounded for joy at meeting an old friend. He brought her mother's casket of jewels which the *saniyasi* in one of his eccentric moods had hidden away, thinking that his Kamala would have the pure joys of true love and home life that are independent of wealth. Ramchander gave her all the news, and when Kamala asked him to go in he begged of her to stay out for some time longer as he had something special to tell her. She wondered what it could be; and then came the great and sudden declaration of his love for her. He pleaded most eloquently :—" It is the land of freedom I want you to come to. Have you not felt the trammels of custom and tradition? Have you not felt the weight of ignorance wearing you down, superstition folding its arms round you and holding you in its bewildering and terrifying grasp? Everything is so dark and dreary for you here. I see it in your eyes. You will be free with me —free as the mountain air, free as the light and sunshine that play around you. Come, Kamala, make up your mind. You were mine before you were born. You were promised to me by your mother. I am tired —tired to death of all the meaningless mummeries of a devotee's life. I have been trying to get at the kernel of truth, at the essence of things, and I have found it not. If you had seen me at the midnight auguries, at the fasts and penances that I have undergone, at the ceremonies and *tapascharias* and endless sacrifices, within the temple and outside, in the dark impenetrable forests and on lonely hill-tops, you would have then known that I have really striven, as none other has, to find the truth. I have followed the *saniyasi*. I have learnt at the feet of the great Arunayadaya. I am acquainted with the *vanaspati* (vegetable) world. I can distil the powerful juice of plants and transplant their subtle vigour into the human frame, but it is all of no avail. It does not bring me any nearer to the object of my pursuit—any nearer to God—the great source of good and evil, the light of the world. Now, Kamala, what say you? We shall create a world of our own and none dare interrupt our joys. I have means at my command of which you know nothing; and love will welcome you in the new world, love such as you have never dreamt of,—my love, my undying love and worship. Accept me and your freedom, and come away with me, and no one will know anything of it."

Kamala looked at him with eyes full of tears, a long melting look, a look capable of piercing even the stoniest heart and bringing forth the inmost floods of sympathy. "Ask me not that," she said, with a shudder. "It is too much for me to think of. Did we wives not die on the funeral pyre in days of old? Did we not court the water and the floods? What has come over us now? My heart beats in response to yours, but betray me not, thou tempting heart. I am ashamed of myself. Despise me and drive me away from thee. Look not on my face. I am the accursed among women. There is something wrong in my nature, and that is why the gods have disgraced me. They have broken the sacred thread of womanhood round my neck; taken my lord and master, and have cursed me. No! What you ask is too much. Leave me as I am, marry a girl more fortunate, and let fortune bless you. You will have happiness and love, love such as you deserve. I am but a broken vessel, fit only to be thrown aside and to be spat on. Ah me! O God! preserve me from this. Something overwhelms me. I see the boundless hills rise before me. They stretch far, far away. They are the emblem of thy power."

"No! It is the power of love," said Ramchander. "Rise, obey its summons. You cannot fight against it. You will pass through waters and floods. Rise, my love, and be mine." And he came nearer and lifted her up. But a cry rang from her heart and she uttered the word, 'Ganesh,' and ran to the house as if mad. It was the cry of a heart pierced to its inmost depth. Her religion, crude as it was, had its victory. She felt that her life would have been an unending remorse and misery; and thus she freed herself once and for ever from the great overpowering influence of the man before her. His love she could not get rid of, for he was true as steel, but it was like sunlight lying on her path and it brightened her life. Ah! it was happiness to know that some one loved her, loved her for her own sake, despised as she was, and degraded in the sight of the little world in which she lived.

Ramchander hid himself in its forest home and only came at stated times to look after his patients, but soon his lonely abode was discovered, and he was besieged by the suffering and the needy, whom he willingly helped. No one suspected his great love: the people merely thought that he was trying to walk in the steps of his master Arunayadaya.

Kamala spent all her money in unselfish works of charity; and her name lives even to this day almost worshipped by the simple folks of the place.

* * * *

It was thus I heard the story of Kamala narrated as I sat by the river banks under a clump of trees. The rude rustic temple of Rohini was at my side. The same old Sivagunga was there, and the same old river rolled on, unmindful of the joys and the sorrows of the lives that were lived by its side. Far in front were a shrine and a chuttram bearing the name of Kamala, who had now become a saint. Her unseen hands still relieve the poor and protect the unfortunate; for she left her fortune for the sole benefit of widows and orphans.